Max

7 Brides for 7 Brothers

LYNN RAYE

NEW YORK TIMES & USA TODAY BESTSELLING AUTHOR

HARRIS

First Edition: November 2016
Library of Congress Cataloging-in-Publication Data

Harris, Lynn Raye
Max (7 Brides for 7 Brothers) / Lynn Raye Harris – 1st ed
ISBN-13: 978-1-941002-21-6

1. Max (7 Brides for 7 Brothers)—Fiction
2. Fiction—Romance
3. Fiction—Contemporary Romance
4. Fiction—Series

Meet the Brannigan brothers—

in the *7 Brides for 7 Brothers* series:

Luke

– Barbara Freethy

Gabe

– Ruth Cardello

Hunter

– Melody Anne

Knox

– Christie Ridgway

Max

– Lynn Raye Harris

James

– Roxanne St. Claire

Finn

– JoAnn Ross

CHAPTER ONE

"What the hell?" Max muttered. He'd just turned into the driveway at Applegate Farm, and it wasn't quite what he'd expected. He kept his foot on the brake of his truck and let his gaze sweep the green grass and white rail fences. It was pretty, if a bit tattered at the edges, but where was the racetrack? And why was there an arena and a horse that was... what? High-stepping like something in a parade, that's what.

The horse was big and flashy, a chestnut with a red mane and tail that were lighter than his coat. There was a rider on his back, a woman with dark brown hair set in a ponytail that bounced as she posted up and down while the horse trotted around the arena.

Max had expected a racetrack with jockeys perched high on horses' backs, exercising them in the morning coolness. The paperwork he'd gotten hadn't said *what* kind of horse farm, but since this was Kentucky, he'd just assumed.

This woman was not a jockey. Her legs were against the horse's sides, not folded up beneath her. The horse's head was high and proud—and there was that prancing thing going on.

1

He didn't know a whole lot about horses, but he knew this wasn't a Thoroughbred racehorse. Which didn't make a lot of sense. Why had his father bought a horse farm that clearly wasn't a racing establishment? Where was the profit in that? Max would have said his father was always looking for the best way to make money at anything, so this made little sense.

"Dammit, Dad, what have you done?"

It had been seven months since his father had died. Colin Brannigan hadn't told a soul that he'd gotten a diagnosis of a rare and aggressive cancer. No, he'd moved himself to the Bahamas and died surrounded by paid caretakers rather than his family. And then he'd left a bunch of envelopes with his handwriting on them, each addressed to one of his seven sons, and asked Aunt Claire to distribute them.

Max's had arrived a couple of months ago now, when he'd finally been Stateside again, but he hadn't opened it right away. He'd stared at it and then propped it on his bedside table with a plan to open it the next day. Enough time had passed that he knew it wasn't money. The estate was in trust and wouldn't be distributed for five years. Typical Dad in many ways.

His brothers had gotten odd bequests—a motorcycle, a lodge, a map, the family house—so he'd expected his would be odd too. He hadn't known how odd until he'd opened the envelope, which hadn't happened the next day since Ian Black had called him with another overseas mission. Max had grabbed his gear and headed out, glad to avoid the contents of the envelope for another few weeks.

When he'd returned a few days ago, he'd had to stop putting off the inevitable. The envelope had contained a deed to a horse farm in Kentucky along with a contract that explained the terms. There was a catch, of course. There was always a catch.

He eased the truck down the driveway and parked beside the barn. It was a big barn, long and painted white. He got out of the truck and surveyed the area. There was a house tucked under some trees a few yards away. It was an older house, brick with white columns, and had that look of genteel Southern decay that you often saw while driving through the old towns of the South.

The farmland was rolling with tall grass that would probably be harvested for hay, and other fields were dotted with horses. He counted ten horses in the pasture and three babies.

The woman on the horse had stopped trotting. He thought she was finished, but then she did something with the reins and the horse started doing something that looked... well, odd. It was almost like a trot, except it wasn't, and the horse looked regal and elegant while doing it.

Still, Max wasn't there to watch horses. He was there to find Elinor Applegate and talk to her about selling this farm. Another woman walked out of the barn just then and stood beside the arena to watch. When she spotted Max, she started walking toward him. He moved in her direction, and when they were close enough, she smiled. She was a pretty blonde, petite, but he suspected she was stronger than she looked if she was out here handling horses.

"Hi, welcome to Applegate Farm. I'm Lacey Hamilton. What can I help you with today?"

Max took her proffered hand. "Max Brannigan. I'm looking for Elinor Applegate."

Lacey's eyes crinkled as her smile widened. "That's El-lie," she said, indicating the woman on the horse. "She'll be a few more minutes if you care to wait."

"Yeah, I'll wait." It wasn't like he had anywhere else to be right now. He'd told Ian he wasn't taking any jobs for the next month or so while he disposed of his *inheritance*. He thought of the day when Knox had opened the storage facili-ty and found out what Dad left him. They'd been on the phone when Knox made the decision to put the key in the lock, and then Knox had e-mailed him after. Now Max was wondering why *he* couldn't have gotten the motorcycle. At least he'd know what to do with that.

"So I'm guessing these aren't racehorses," he said as he watched the horse in the arena fly around it, still doing that high-stepping gait.

Lacey laughed. "Definitely not. Ellie raises and trains American saddlebreds." She nodded toward the arena. "That's a rack if you're wondering."

After a moment of surprise, he decided that Lacey wasn't discussing Ellie's chest. "It's different, that's for sure."

"It is. But it's beautiful, right?" Lacey whooped then, surprising him, but she was yelling at Ellie and the horse as they flew by. "Yeah, boy!"

Max couldn't deny her statement. There was something fluid and graceful about the way the horse moved—and the way the rider sat up straight and tall. "Yep, it's amazing. I've never seen that before."

Lacey smiled. "You came on a good day then."

Ellie brought the horse to a stop and then bent over and hugged his neck. The horse stood there blowing and sweat-

4

ing, his mouth working the bit while she petted him. Then she sat up and gathered the reins loosely. The horse started walking toward the exit.

"Come on into the barn," Lacey said.

Max followed her inside. He'd ridden horses a couple of times growing up. There'd been that summer when his parents had taken them all to the Algoma Resort and he and his brothers took a lesson from the trainer there. The biggest surprise had been Mom. She hadn't needed a lesson at all. She'd gotten on that horse and taken off like she'd been born to it.

Max could still remember the smell of the stables, that sweet-hay-and-horse smell that had filled his days. They'd been happy days with his family—before his mother died and everything changed.

Walking into the stables now, he was hit with that same smell. It was a happy smell—and a sad one because it reminded him, forcefully, that both his parents were gone and he'd never be that carefree little boy he'd once been. Hell, as if that was the only reason he'd never be carefree again.

He shook off his dark thoughts as Lacey chatted beside him. Now was not the time.

"Hey, Ellie, got a visitor for you," Lacey said as Ellie strode down the aisle, leading the horse. "I'll take Champ."

Max did a bit of a double take at the size of the beast — and the diminutive form of the woman standing beside him.

"Thanks," Ellie said, handing the reins to Lacey and patting the horse on the neck. "You were a good boy today. Extra carrots for you."

Max moved out of the aisle as Lacey led the horse past him, then turned and faced Elinor Applegate. She was small, about five-four or so, and when she smiled his heart did a little skip thing that was completely unexpected.

"Hi there," she said. "I'm Ellie—what can I help you with today?"

"I'm Max." He expected her to react to his name, but she didn't. She just kept looking at him with a smile on her face in spite of the fact her eyebrows drew together for a second.

She didn't know him. *Dammit, Dad, what are you playing at?*

"It's nice to meet you, Max. Are you here about the HVAC? I called for service yesterday, but I thought Roger wasn't sending anyone out until tomorrow."

"No," he said, and she frowned slightly. "I'm Max Brannigan. Colin Brannigan's son."

⊌

Ellie's mouth went dry, and her heart beat a little faster. She'd known this day was coming, but she'd kept hoping as the months went by since Colin's death that it wouldn't come until later this year. She only needed a few more months, and then Champ might just save her bacon—and the farm's bacon.

But if a Brannigan was here now, then time was running out. She tried to keep the smile on her face as she gazed at him. Holy cow, he was tall. And seriously beautiful. Dark hair, silver eyes, and the kind of muscles that said he could haul hay and not even feel worn out at the end of the day.

Not that she imagined the son of a media tycoon had ever hauled hay. Or gotten dirty for that matter.

"I'm sorry for your loss," she said, bringing her mind back to the topic at hand. "Your father was a good man."

He looked momentarily surprised. "Thank you."

"Can I offer you something to drink? Sweet tea? Lemonade? Water?"

She didn't know what else to do with him. Plus she wanted to stall for time since she was pretty sure she didn't want to hear whatever he'd come here for. His brows drew down for a second as his gaze raked over her. She knew her face was red from exertion, and she could feel the sweat dripping between her breasts. She looked like hell while he looked like something that had walked off one of his father's movie sets.

"I'm fine, but you look like you could use something," he said.

Yep, she looked like hell.

"Come on up to the house." Not that she wanted him inside her home, but she wanted him in her barn even less. He could take all this away from her—or so she assumed. She didn't know the terms of Colin's will or who got what —she only knew she hadn't gotten her farm back. Not that she'd expected a man she'd only met once would leave it to her, of course. The Brannigans owned it and could do what they wanted.

She tried not to imagine the worst as she trudged up to the house with Max at her side. He didn't say anything as they walked, and she didn't either. How could she speak when her throat was tight and her mind conjured the worst?

She'd beg him. That's what she'd do. Just a few more months. Just until Louisville and the World's Championship Horse Show at the end of August. That was all she needed. She had no pride when it came to her horses and her farm. She'd do whatever it took to keep them.

Stop it, Ellie. You don't know why he's here. He could just be checking on a Brannigan investment.

Yes, he could—but that wasn't any better, was it? As an investment, Applegate Farm sucked. She pulled in a deep breath as she stepped up onto the stone porch and reached for the door. Max beat her to it, pulling the screen door wide so she had only to open the big wooden door to the house.

She tried not to focus on his presence behind her, on the heat and size of him as he stood so close. The door swung open, and she stepped into blessed coolness. The house was old, dating from around the turn of the century, but at least Momma had invested in air-conditioning when she'd had the money.

"Come on in and have a seat. I'll just be a second." She showed Max to the settee in the living room and then tried not to think about how he dwarfed it as he sat down. His legs were long, and his arms were packed with muscle. Not the kind of muscle that came from a gym, though she imagined some of it did, but the kind that came from hard work.

She hadn't realized it when she'd been looking at him in the barn, but it was definitely a shock now. She'd have said a Brannigan didn't need to work a day in his life to be comfortable and fed. It made her wonder what kind of hard labor he must have done to get that way. Probably something like rock climbing or an extreme sport. Hadn't she read that one of his brothers was an extreme athlete?

Yes. Luke Brannigan.

Max lifted one eyebrow, and Ellie dragged her gaze away, mortified that she'd been staring. "Sure you don't want anything?"

"I'm fine."

Boy was he. "Make yourself comfortable. I'll be right back."

She marched into the kitchen and tugged open the ancient refrigerator. After she grabbed a bottle of water, she rolled it over her forehead and cheeks before twisting off the cap and taking a drink. She stood at the sink, staring out at the rolling fields and the horses grazing peacefully, tails swishing, before she drew herself up and headed back to the living room.

Max looked up as she entered, and she forced herself not to react to his pretty face. Not this time. She sank onto a chair opposite and set her water on the side table. Then she pasted on a smile.

"I don't suppose you're here for a social call, so if you'd like to tell me what this is about, we can get on with it."

Take the bull by the horns, Ellie. That's what Momma always used to say whenever Ellie had hesitated over something. Typically, Momma was talking about a training a horse. Hesitation was defeat when dealing with horses. And maybe it was with this man too.

Max Brannigan stretched his arm along the back of the settee, muscles bunching and smoothing as he did so. Ellie's mouth went dry.

"No, not really. My father left me this farm, and I came out here to see what kind of operation you have. I have to admit I'm disappointed."

Ellie felt his comment like a blow. It also raised her hackles. "I'm sorry we're not up to your standards, Mr. Brannigan."

A flush of anger and embarrassment rolled through her as she thought of what he must think sitting in her run-down living room. The house was old and historic but in desperate need of repair. Except work took money, and that was something she didn't have. She should have never invited him inside. Now he was here and she had to endure knowing that he was looking down his nose at her and her home.

He frowned. "I'm sorry, that came out wrong. I meant that I don't understand why my father bought this farm. You're raising saddlebreds, according to Miss Hamilton, and I fail to see why he would have been interested in something so, well, decorative. I expected racehorses. Something that could earn money."

Ellie's pulse was a wild thing. As if she hadn't heard it all before. Saddlebreds were useless. Flighty. Silly. What could anyone possibly see in these horses? They got so little respect outside the saddlebred community. They weren't Olympic horses, weren't racehorses, weren't workhorses—she'd heard it all, and it just wasn't true. Saddlebreds were versatile, intelligent. Hell, they used to be cavalry horses during the Civil War—how was that decorative?

Still, if she looked at it objectively, she could understand his confusion. He wasn't a horseman, and racehorses made more sense for a tycoon like Colin Brannigan to have invested in.

Ellie cleared her throat, uncertain how much to say. "My mother and yours were good friends. When my mother needed an investor, your dad was there. She offered the farm as collateral, and we've been paying the loan back faithfully ever since."

It was much more complicated than that, but Ellie wasn't telling him any more than he needed to know. Some things were too private, and too heartbreaking, to discuss with strangers. Even a stranger who was the son of the man who'd helped out at a very bad time.

"I didn't know that. He didn't explain it in the paperwork he left me."

Ellie twisted her hands together in her lap. "I *will* pay you back, Mr. Brannigan. I send in the money every month, or as much of it as I can—and I hope to buy the loan outright in the near future."

He was frowning. "How soon?"

She hesitated. It was nothing more than hope and speculation at this point. "I-I don't know. A few months. Maybe a year."

If she was lucky. If Champ kept working the way he was going and she won the five-gaited stake at Louisville in August. If someone offered to buy him once he did, though the prospect of losing such a talented colt hurt on many levels. So many ifs to get where she needed to go.

Max's frown grew deeper. "I'm not interested in running a horse farm, Miss Applegate. You can buy the loan back now—or we can discuss liquidating the property and settling the debt."

CHAPTER TWO

She was gazing at him with a deer-in-the-headlights look. Max didn't like the way his gut twisted over the look on her face, but dammit, he wasn't running a charity. He had plans of his own. He wasn't sitting around and waiting for her to get the money or for the terms of the contract to expire. He'd done his time in the trenches, fought his battles, and it was time he did something for himself for a change. Past time.

James and Gabe were tycoons in their own right, but he'd never been interested in running a business. That had changed in the past few months. He was tired of busting his ass for someone else's vision. He had his own vision. A high-end protection firm—diplomats, billionaires, captains of industry, the kind of people who needed a certain kind of protection, especially when they were traveling in hot spots around the world. He and his people would provide it.

This was something he could recruit his old SEAL buddies for, a way to give back and give jobs to veterans who couldn't quite leave behind the danger and intrigue of life lived on the edge. Not many people knew what it was like to live a high-octane life and then come to a full stop. But he did. The men he worked with did. That's why they took crazy jobs in war-torn locations. Why they fought for the highest bidder.

He thought he had a better way, but he needed the money to get started. He could ask James or Gabe, sure, but neither of them had asked for help from anyone when they'd started out. No way was he going to be the brother who needed an assist starting his own company. In a family as driven as his, he'd never live it down. And then there was the fact they didn't actually know what he did. If he asked for money, they'd insist on knowing everything.

It was enough that they thought he was working security in volatile places. Hell, maybe they suspected he was a contract soldier, but no one ever asked and he never confirmed it. And he wasn't about to go into detail for anyone. Maybe Finn, if Finn ever wanted to know, because his baby brother was a Navy pilot and understood what it was like to serve.

Ellie Applegate was looking at him like he'd just kicked a puppy. It didn't make him feel good. He thought of the clause in the contract that stated he had to visit Applegate Farm before he could sell it, and his aggravation at his father grew.

"Liquidating the property? What does that mean?"

She sounded very calm and unemotional, which he suspected meant she was anything but. He also suspected she knew precisely what he meant. And yeah, he felt like an ass for even suggesting it. But he needed the money. He had quite a bit of his own from all the foreign jobs since he'd left the military—but it still wasn't enough to get his business going and employ the people he needed.

"It means we can sell the farm and discharge your debt. You go your way, I go mine—"

"And where would I go? You're talking about my home." There were two bright splotches in her cheeks, and he realized she was definitely not calm. It also occurred to him that she wasn't exactly aware of the terms of the contract he'd gotten from his father.

"You wouldn't be homeless, Miss Applegate. You get half the proceeds from the sale—which would probably be substantial considering this property is located so close to Lexington."

There had been a sign as he'd driven through on the way here that proclaimed Lexington as the Horse Capital of the World. Good for her. Good for him.

She looked stunned. That was the only word for it. Her pretty mouth dropped open and her green eyes widened. He had the oddest urge to sweep her up and kiss her, but no way was he giving in to that urge. He had no doubt where she'd aim her knee if he even tried. He'd just watched this wisp of a woman handle a thousand-plus-pound animal like it was a puppy—and he wasn't about to test her reflexes anywhere near his balls.

"I... Half the proceeds? Why?"

Max was beginning to get pissed. Not at her, but at the old man. His father had left him a hell of a mess—and Colin certainly hadn't told Elinor Applegate a bit of what he'd planned. Max could keep it from her, but it wouldn't change the terms or what had to be done.

He hadn't understood any of it when he'd pored over the documents, but he'd figured there was no way Elinor

Applegate wouldn't want half the money right now. He was beginning to wonder about that assessment, however.

"It's in the contract my father left me. If we sell right now, you get half the money. All we have to do is call in an agent, get it appraised, and get it on the market."

And since he didn't expect any of that to happen fast, he'd spend some time here as his father had requested.

Her fingers had curled into fists. "This is my home. I don't want to sell it, though I don't suppose that's up to me, is it? You come in here all arrogant and certain of yourself, and you want to sell my farm because you don't know what it means to love something so much you'd sacrifice everything you have rather than part with it." She snorted. "You rich boys are all the same. Think you can have whatever you want and to hell with the consequences to anyone else."

Max hadn't been called a rich boy in so many years that he had to do a double take. He'd been on his own, paving his way in the world, for over a decade now. He'd served his country with distinction, and he'd gone through more hell than this woman could imagine. Rich? Not yet. Entitled? Hardly. Not to mention that her tone pissed him the fuck off.

"You don't know a thing about me, Miss Applegate," he said coolly. "Not a goddamn thing. And I don't know a thing about you, but I'm not blind. You have nothing more than some fancy prancing horses here, and while I don't know much about horses, I'm pretty sure those can't bring in much money. Not like racehorses. I suggest you cut your losses while you can and find a smaller place where you can keep a couple of animals and continue doing whatever it is you do with them."

"Whatever it is—" She shook her head as if to clear it. Then she stood, her entire body vibrating with anger. And, yeah, it was wrong of him, but there was something slightly exhilarating about her anger. Her eyes flashed fire and her chin quivered before she clamped down on her reaction. "You need to leave now, Mr. Brannigan. Get off my property and stay off. You can send your realtors and you can list my farm, but I'm not cooperating with any of it until I call my lawyer and find out exactly what you can and can't do. I have a mortgage and I'm not in default—and I'm not accepting your word as the final authority just yet."

Max towered over her as he rose from the couch. "First of all, it's *my* property. Second, I've got some bad news for you, sweetheart," he said, and her eyes narrowed. Whether it was the bad news or the sarcastic endearment causing it, he didn't know. And he really didn't care. "Or maybe it's good news to you. I can't sell this farm for a year from the date of my father's death without your agreement—"

She sucked in a breath, and he knew she was surprised. But he kept going before she could respond.

"—but I also own this place. So long as I do, I'm not staying in a hotel."

Outrage shone from her eyes. "You can't stay here."

He took a step toward her. She didn't flinch or back down. He admired that about her. It fired his blood, made his heart beat faster. What was it about this woman that got beneath his skin? He didn't know, but no way was he letting her win this round.

"Yes, I *fucking* can."

U

"Here's your room," Ellie said, throwing open the door to the large bedroom on the ground floor of the house. She was mightily pissed but handling it well. Or so she thought. Maybe she'd thrown the door open a little hard. It had slammed into the doorstop with enough force to send it careening back again. She caught it and stepped aside to let him enter.

The entire house needed updating, but this room probably needed it most of all. The plaster was cracked, the walls were yellow, the floors still had 1970s shag carpeting on top of the hardwood, and there was no overhead lighting. The windows had been painted shut years ago, and she hadn't managed to get them open yet. No time, really. It was also hot because she'd shut off the vents to keep her costs down.

The bed was old and the mattress had seen better days. She folded her arms over her chest and refused to feel even the tiniest bit guilty as Max walked into the room and dropped his duffel bag. A duffel instead of Louis Vuitton suitcases. Yeah, that had been a surprise. He might be rich, but he didn't quite act like it.

Except for the part where he wanted to sell her home. That thought worked to harden her heart and erase any possible sympathy as he turned around inside the room and studied the walls. He'd insisted he was staying, so she'd given him a room. The worst room.

"Saved the best for me, huh?" he said softly.

She sniffed. "Yep, nothing but the best for you, Mr. Brannigan."

"I think you should call me Max if we're going to be

17

living together, don't you?" One handsome eyebrow quirked up, and she felt a little ache begin in the pit of her stomach. Why oh why did he have to be so damned pretty?

"Max it is. I'm sorry there's no en suite bath here." No, she wasn't. The more uncomfortable he was, the better. "There's a half bath in the hall, but you'll have to go upstairs for a shower."

"And will I be sharing the bathroom with you, Ellie?"

Her skin prickled at his use of her name. It was the first time he'd called her anything besides Miss Applegate. She began to think maybe she'd made a mistake in accepting his invitation to call him Max. Because he was now going to call her Ellie, and the way he said her name, all deep and growly, did things to her insides that she'd rather not think about.

"Thankfully, no. I have my own bathroom."

She'd been embarrassed earlier when she thought of the run-down state of the house and having him in it, but now she hoped it worked to run him off. A couple of nights on that lumpy old mattress in this musty old room and he'd surely decide to head off to a fancy hotel in Lexington and park his privileged ass there for the duration.

She hoped.

"Convenient."

Her temper spiked at his sarcastic tone. "If you think I'm giving up my room so you can have an en suite, *milord*, you're crazy."

He held up both hands. "Nope, didn't think that at all. Just stating a fact."

Like hell he hadn't been needling her.

"You'll have to do your own shopping," she said. "There's not much in the fridge, and I don't cook."

"I'll need a key."

"I'll get you a key the next time I go into town." She had a spare in the kitchen drawer since she couldn't afford a housekeeper anymore.

He glanced around the room again. "Wouldn't you like to have something smaller and more modern? A place where you don't have to worry about what might break next or how much it's going to cost to update a room?"

Her heart froze. "This house has been in my family for four generations. No, I don't want something smaller or more modern. If you feel your accommodations aren't modern enough, you can go find a hotel. Or update the damn room yourself."

She had a strong urge to slam the door and storm off, but she managed not to do it. Max had arched an eyebrow again. She wanted to march over there and smooth it back down with her finger. Then maybe she'd skim his strong jaw before dropping her hand and—

What? No! No way in hell did she want to touch Max Brannigan. Just because she hadn't had a date in the two years since Momma died was no reason to start having fantasies about this man. He was all wrong. Totally wrong. She'd dated a rich boy in college, and she wanted nothing to do with that kind of entitled jerk again.

Rich boys cared about themselves and their toys, nothing more. This one was even worse. He already came from a supremely wealthy family, and yet he wanted to sell her farm so he could have even more money. Colin Brannigan had been worth billions. Even if his seven sons had split the fortune, it was still a lot of money. More than most people would see in a lifetime. Hell, if Max never got a penny from

Applegate Farm, he wouldn't miss it. How much money was enough for one man anyway?

"The accommodations are fine," he bit out. "But I'll need that key today, not whenever you get around to it."

She lifted her chin. "I want to see where it says you need my permission to sell."

He frowned. "Why?"

"Because I don't trust you. Because you might sell it anyway and then what could I do about it?" She shook her head. "No key until you show me."

She thought he might blow up, but then he laughed suddenly and her insides warmed at the sound. Which made her mightily sore with herself.

Do. Not. Smile. At. This. Man.

"You can read the entire contract. Call your lawyer if you like. I'll have my dad's attorney fax over a copy. I own Applegate Farm, but I can't sell it until September—unless you agree. After that, I can do what I want."

Her heart squeezed painfully. He owned it lock, stock, and barrel. But she still had time. Somehow it didn't make her feel any better. "Do I still have the right to buy back my loan?"

Because it occurred to her that if Colin Brannigan was dead and Max Brannigan owned the farm outright, perhaps it was up to him how much money she had to come up with. She hoped she was wrong. Prayed she was wrong.

He stared at her for a beat too long, and her stomach did a slow sink into her toes.

"Your loan is null and void, Ellie. You'll have to buy the farm at a price I set... up to the appraisal amount."

CHAPTER THREE

Max raked a hand through his hair as he stood in the center of the room Ellie had shown him to. She'd disappeared approximately two minutes ago, her face going white before she'd lifted that stubborn chin and told him she had work to do. Then she'd faded away and he'd been left standing there, feeling like an asshole.

He took out his phone and called up his list of favorites. Then he hit Knox's number and waited. Knox answered on the second ring.

"Hey, man," his brother said. "You back in country?"

"Yeah. Got back a few days ago."

Knox didn't wait to go in for the kill. "Did you open the envelope?"

"Sure did. Standing in the middle of my inheritance now."

He thought his brother snickered. "What did you get?"

"Nothing as cool as your Indian."

"Well, I ended up with something even cooler than that, don't forget."

"Yeah, I know." Knox had met Erin when he'd gotten the Indian out of storage and gone for a ride up the Pacific coast. Somehow his brother had ended up falling in love. Not at all what Max would have expected from Knox, aka the guy who always had a ready smile and a new woman on his arm whenever Max saw him. The idea of falling in love and settling down was so foreign to Max that he couldn't comprehend how it had happened to his brother. *Brothers,* since it seemed as if Luke, Hunter, Gabe, and Knox were all in committed relationships now.

Mind-boggling.

Max remembered his parents being happy, but that had ended when his mother died. His father threw himself into work and was never happy again. Not that Max had realized that when he'd been growing up, but he knew it now. Love had broken his father. It would break his brothers too if they let it, and there was nothing any of them could do to stop it.

But love would not break him. Of that he was certain. You had to have a heart to fall in love—and his had been hardened beyond repair in the hell of war.

"So what is it?" Knox asked. "What was the grand prize in your mystery envelope?"

"A horse farm. In Kentucky."

They both knew that Mom and Aunt Claire had grown up in Kentucky, but they'd never been there themselves. It occurred to Max that he didn't actually know where in Kentucky his mother was from. Apparently it was somewhere around here if she'd known Ellie's mother. He'd have to call Aunt Claire and ask her.

"Wow. Never knew Dad was into horses. Any Kentucky Derby winners in your future? Should Erin get a hat?"

Max went over to the window—the rippled window because the glass was old—and looked out at the bluegrass.

"Not unless they change the rules to allow prancing down the homestretch."

"Uh... what?" Knox sounded as confused as Max had felt when he'd driven up and seen Ellie on that horse earlier.

"Saddlebreds," he said. "They prance. Pretty enough, but useless. No racehorses. No purses. Nothing but prancers who like to eat and take up space."

Knox was laughing now. Max tried not to feel annoyed about it.

"Hey, you don't really know they're useless. What if there's money in these horses? Surely people don't raise them for the hell of it."

Max put a hand to his forehead and rubbed. "If there was, don't you think the world would have heard of it? There are pictures in the house and barn. People wearing fussy hats and long coats, sitting on top of horses and looking like they have sticks up their asses. I seriously don't think there's money in this, Knox. Dad left me a fucking useless horse farm."

And a woman who definitely did not want to cooperate in disposing of said farm.

Knox wasn't laughing now. "Dude, I'm sorry. But don't you think there's something more there? Something Dad wanted you to know?"

"If he wanted me to know that life is hard and we don't always get what we want, well, I already knew that. If he wanted me to know that women are unreasonable and emotional, I knew that too."

"There's a woman?" Max could hear Knox's curiosity.

"Yeah, there's a woman. Her name's Ellie. Her mother was friends with ours. Dad loaned her mother money."

"I take it her mother isn't there anymore?"

"Ellie's was the only name on the contract Dad left me. I assume her mother's gone, but I didn't ask."

"Maybe you should."

"Yeah, I should." She'd expressed sympathy for his loss, and he hadn't said a word about hers. If there was a loss. Maybe her mother had retired to Florida and was lying on a beach somewhere. But if she had, wouldn't she be named on the contract as one of the beneficiaries of the proceeds?

Max blew out a breath. "I own the farm, but I can't sell it for a year after Dad's death. Not unless Ellie agrees to sell. And she won't. Not anytime soon."

"So don't sell. Live the life of a gentleman farmer. Raise horses and bale hay for the next few months. See what the fuss is all about."

Max pulled the phone from his ear and stared at it for a second. Knox was losing his damn mind. No other excuse for it since Knox had spent his time wandering up the Pacific coast and falling for a woman who ran a yoga studio. Knox might be capable of leisure, but Max damn sure wasn't. If he wasn't doing a HALO jump out of an airplane at thirty-five thousand feet in the middle of the night over enemy territory, then he was on the front lines with his guns and his buddies and they were making a *difference* in the world.

He did not do idle. He did not do gentleman farmer.

Except you just moved into this house, didn't you?

Yeah, but that was temporary. His father might have wanted him to stay here, but he'd done it mostly to prove to Ellie Applegate that she didn't control what went on around here anymore. She definitely didn't control him. Just as soon as she got sick of him being in her hair, they'd come to an arrangement.

"I think you know better than that, Knox," he said coolly.

Knox laughed. "You never know until you try. You might like slowing down for a change."

The hell he would.

U

Ellie sat across from her friend and watched as Janet flipped through the pages of the contract the Brannigan family lawyer had faxed over. Janet was an attorney, but she wasn't Ellie's attorney because Ellie couldn't afford that kind of help. But she was a friend, and as a friend she'd agreed to look at the document *pro bono*. She slipped her glasses off and looked up. She wasn't smiling.

"It's pretty straightforward, Ellie. Max Brannigan owns the farm and any horses registered to the farm. He can sell, but only with your agreement—and he only needs that for a year, which is up in September, unfortunately. After that he can do what he wants with it. Right now you get half the proceeds from a sale... After that, you get nothing unless he decides to give it to you."

Ellie sat back in the overstuffed leather club chair in front of Janet's desk and felt as if someone had whomped the air right out of her. "That's not your standard agreement, is it?"

"No, it's definitely not."

"Is it legal?"

"It appears to be, yes. It was Colin Brannigan's property to do with as he wished. He loaned your mother money, but they had no formal contract. All they had was an IOU that she signed and a schedule of payments. If Max wants to accept that, he can. He doesn't have to." She stuck one end of her glasses into the corner of her mouth for a second. "You could take him to court and try to get him to adhere to the original IOU—but it would be expensive and you'd probably lose. He has the deed to the property, and he has the right to dispose of it."

"With my agreement."

"For one year from the date of his father's death, yes."

Ellie scrubbed a hand over her head. "Isn't that odd? Why a year? Why give me half?"

Janet shrugged. "Colin Brannigan was from California. They're all weird out there."

Ellie snorted. "No kidding."

"So how are the horses registered?"

"They're all in the farm's name. Except for Champ. He's mine. A birthday present from Momma before she got sick." Thank God. She shivered at the thought of how badly this could go for her if Champ belonged to Applegate Farm and therefore to Max.

"That's good." Janet leaned forward, a sudden gleam in her eye. "So what's Max like, hmm? Colin might have been an older man, but he wasn't a bad-looking one."

"How do you know?"

Janet smiled and opened a desk drawer. When she plopped a handful of celebrity magazines on the desk, Ellie gaped. Janet shrugged again. "It's mindless entertainment. I like reading about all the outrageousness in Hollywood." She leaned back in her seat. "Anyway, Colin Brannigan owned Skylight Pictures. He was in the rags a lot until he died. Tragic, poor man."

"Cancer, wasn't it?"

"Aggressive and sudden, or so the news said. He was only sixty-seven."

Ellie thought of Max sitting in her living room and felt a pang of sympathy for him. She knew from experience that it wasn't easy to lose a parent. And though she couldn't fathom Max's life as a Brannigan or understand what his relationship with his father had been, she still couldn't imagine it was an easy thing to absorb. Especially as suddenly as Colin had passed.

"So," Janet said, interrupting her thoughts. "Is he hand-some?"

Ellie hoped the current of heat flaring to life inside her wasn't making her cheeks red. If it was, Janet very politely didn't comment.

"I suppose he is. If you like that kind of thing."

Janet guffawed. "Girl, who doesn't?"

Ellie's mouth twisted. "All right, yes, he's freaking gorgeous. Tall, dark hair, gray eyes, and muscles that go on for days. Too bad he's an arrogant jackass."

"So many of them are, darling."

"Isn't that the truth?"

"He's moved in, huh?"

"He won't stay long. I put him in the worst room in the house. I predict he'll be gone by tomorrow—Saturday at the latest. He won't stay there when he can move to the Gratz Park Inn or the Castle Post and be waited on hand and foot."

Janet turned the contract and pushed it toward her. "You might as well keep this for reference. I know it's not what you wanted, but at least you have some time. If Champ wins like you hope, you can sell him and offer to buy Max out."

Ellie frowned as she folded the contract in half. "Yeah."

Janet's face creased with sympathy. "I thought that's what you wanted, Ellie. You've been working your ass off to turn that horse into the best five-gaited colt in the country."

She stuffed the contract into her purse and folded her arms. God, she was ridiculous sometimes. "It is what I want. But I'll miss him, Janet. I'll miss what could have been if I kept him for breeding."

Applegate Farm was once known for their superior stock. She wanted it to be that way again. She wanted to restore their reputation and prove they still had what it took to succeed. And she wanted to prove that she was as good a horse trainer as her mother had once been. Before her mother had gotten sick. Before she'd lost it all.

"He's a million-dollar horse, El. You may never get another one."

"Only if he wins," Ellie said, her throat tight. Which he needed to do in the next couple of weeks at the first show of the season and then keep on doing all spring and summer long.

"You'll be fine. You're an Applegate."

But I'm not Momma, she wanted to say. *I don't know what I'm doing the way she did.*

"Thanks."

"You wait and see, Ellie. I might not be much of a horsewoman, but I know what I'm talking about."

U

Ellie turned into her long driveway and prayed for the strength to deal with whatever waited for her up at the house. She'd spent a couple of hours with Janet. They'd gone to lunch at Malone's in Lexington, and then she'd stopped by the tack store on the way home and picked up a gallon of Absorbine liniment to rub the horses down after their workouts. As she came out from beneath the stand of trees that shielded the view of the barns and house, she put her foot on the brake and stared.

There was a dumpster. Beside her house. And there was a man hauling carpeting out the door and tossing it into the dumpster. She shook her head, certain she must be hallucinating, but the scene didn't change. She pressed the gas and went up to the house, stopping and jumping from the truck as Max came out the door with another wad of carpeting.

"What the hell are you doing?" she demanded.

He stopped and looked at her. He was wearing a clingy white T-shirt, of all the damn things, and sweat glistened on his arms and face. He had on gloves and a face mask. His dark hair was damp, and his chest was broad, and her heart was beating entirely too fast.

He hauled the carpet to the dumpster and chucked it inside. Then he faced her, dirt streaking his shirt, and eyes flashing fire as he pulled the mask down.

"I'm ripping up that awful shag carpeting. What's it look like?"

She strode over and stopped in front of him, fury pumping into her. "I was gone for three hours. *Three hours*. And

29

you've rented a dumpster and started tearing out the carpet? What gives you the right?"

He grinned, and her heart did that skip-jump thing she was beginning to expect. "You did, sugar. *Update the damn room yourself.* Remember that?"

Oh, for heaven's sake. Ellie closed her eyes for a second. Dammit, she *had* said that. She'd been angry—and no way had she thought he'd do it. Maybe she should have known better.

"I do now."

"Cheer up, Ellie. You aren't the one doing the work or footing the bill."

"Well, thank God for small favors."

He laughed. "Sarcasm? Why am I not surprised?"

She sniffed. "If you want to renovate, go for it. But just remember, that's the room you're staying in. If you make it uninhabitable for yourself in the interim, you'll have nowhere to go but the barn. Or a hotel."

"I think I can manage. I'm not refinishing the floors today. Only ripping out the carpet."

He shoved a hand through his damp hair. It stuck up in places, and he was still sexy in spite of it. Lord have mercy, her libido did not need to flare up now. *Over two years, Ellie. That's a long damn time.*

Yes it was, but so what? There would be time for men later. Once she'd turned Champ into the sensation he was going to be. She hadn't missed having a man in her life at all. She still didn't miss it—except this one made her think there were parts of having a man around that she might have been missing after all.

"Well, keep it quiet. I don't want to hear you banging around in there when I'm trying to sleep."

He snorted. "It's not even three in the afternoon yet. What makes you think I'll still be doing this tonight?"

She cocked a hip and put a hand on it. "Do you have any idea what you're doing? I'd have thought a rich tycoon's son would hire people to do the dirty work, not get dirty himself."

He shook his head slowly. It was a mocking gesture, and she felt the weight of it like a stone in her gut. Okay, so she was doing a lot of assuming here. But he hadn't shown her any differently.

Isn't that what he's doing right now?

"I'm not a stranger to hard work if that's what you're thinking. Some parents with money give their children everything and teach them the value of nothing. Some give their children nothing and teach them the value of everything. I'll let you guess which one my father was."

So maybe being born with a silver spoon wasn't everything. She thought of her mother and her stories about growing up with Kathleen Brannigan—who wasn't a Brannigan then, of course. Kathleen had loved horses too. They'd spent summers riding as much as they could and working in the stable under Ellie's grandfather in order to learn everything about training horses.

Ellie's mother had been born to it, but Kathleen had worked hard to earn the right to sit at the feet of a master. She'd been good with horses, Momma said. She had good hands and a good seat, and she might have gone far if she hadn't answered a different calling in life.

And then she'd died in a car accident far too young. She'd left behind a husband and seven sons. Momma had cried for days when she'd heard the news. Ellie had only been five, but she remembered the time Momma had gotten upset about her friend. Ellie hadn't quite understood why it was a bad thing that Kathleen Brannigan had gone to heaven, but of course she understood that kind of loss now.

She'd just assumed that Kathleen's children had been spoiled by the money and privilege, but she didn't really know that. She should apologize to him, but the words got stuck in her throat. She was certainly putting her foot in her mouth today, wasn't she?

"Speaking of hard work, I have horses to feed," she said. "I'd better get to it."

He frowned for a second. "Do you need help?"

She started to reject his offer, but something stopped her. Miguel wasn't here this afternoon to help. If she accepted Max's offer, she'd get done that much faster and she could move on to other chores. She might not like him much, but she didn't have to like him to accept his help. "If you've got a few moments, yeah, that'd be great."

He peeled off his gloves and tucked them into the pocket of his jeans. "Then let's get going."

CHAPTER FOUR

Max wasn't sure why he'd offered to help feed horses. He walked down to the barn with Ellie, all the while trying not to think about how her hair hung thick and shiny to the middle of her back or how her shirt clung to the curves of her body, emphasizing her breasts. He hadn't seen her when she'd left the house earlier, so he didn't know what she'd been wearing.

Now he was having a hard time thinking about anything else. Clingy black shirt with decorative buttons on the sleeves, a pair of faded jeans, and black boots that zipped up the center before disappearing beneath her jeans. She was curvy in all the right places, and she was small enough that he still had trouble believing she could handle horses the size of the one she'd been riding earlier.

She walked into the open barn and headed for a room where she slid the door open and started dipping grain from a covered bin, tossing it into a wheelbarrow. When it was full, she rolled it into the aisle.

"You can grab an armful of hay and follow me."

If the barn had been tranquil before, now it was alive with the sound of horses nickering for food. Ellie pulled up to the first stall, scooped up some grain, and dumped it into the feed bucket through an opening in the stall.

She came over and took some hay from him, showing him the amount. "Give this much to each horse, okay?"

"Got it."

She opened the stall and tossed the hay inside, then went down the line, scooping grain into buckets while he followed and dropped hay into each stall. He had to go back a couple of times for more, but when it was done he calculated that they'd fed twelve horses.

"What about the ones in the pasture?"

"They've been fed already. They don't need as much with the grass."

Ellie rolled the wheelbarrow back into the feed room. A cat came running from somewhere, and she cooed to it before dumping cat food into a bowl and scratching its back while it ate, purring loud enough to be heard across the room where Max stood.

Ellie looked up and smiled. He liked her smile, but it faded quicker than he wanted it to.

"Thanks for helping."

"You're welcome. Wasn't too hard."

She came toward him and he stepped out of the way while she pulled the door closed.

"What about the cat?"

"Caesar?" She pointed to the walls that didn't go all the way to the roof. "He'll scale that wall in half a second flat. Then he'll stroll along on the rafters for a while before he decides to come down."

Max gazed down the length of the wide aisle that went from one end of the barn to the other. "You have room for more horses."

"Forty stalls. They were full at one time."

"But not any longer."

Her gaze clouded for a second. "No, not any longer." She shrugged. "The horse business is tough. There are highs and lows, like with anything. Horses are a luxury, and they're typically the first to go when times are rough. Keeping a horse for your kid costs more than piano lessons or karate or most other sports. It's a no-brainer when it's time to economize."

He looked at the nameplates on the closest stalls. Applegate's Highland Flame. Applegate's Bronze Beauty. Applegate's No Regrets.

"You bred all these horses?"

She followed his gaze. "Many of them, yes. My mother had a gift for figuring out which bloodlines to cross for the results she wanted. At one time, Applegate horses were prized for their sensibility and smooth action. You can still find Applegate's Cavalier in the bloodlines of many of today's champions."

She walked over to the stall that said Applegate's No Regrets. "This is Champ. He's the future of Applegate Farm."

Max went over and peered into the stall. A handsome horse was busy devouring his food, the scent of sweet grain and molasses permeating the air as he ate. It was the horse she'd been riding when Max arrived.

He put a hand on one of the bars, and the horse lifted his nose and nudged Max's fingers before diving into his bowl again. It was unexpected and oddly comforting in a way. Like when he'd been a kid and they'd gone on that vacation a few months before Mom died. He'd liked feeding the horses carrots. Mom had shown him how to do it.

"Hold it like this, Max. Curl your fist around the bottom—there, like that."

The horse had taken half the carrot in the first bite. In the second, Mom helped him hold on while the horse took more. And then she'd had him lay his palm flat with the remaining piece on top. The horse nuzzled his palm, soft lips tickling as the carrot disappeared.

"He's a sweetie," Ellie was saying. "Gentle for a stud."

Max fixed his gaze on her again, and she cocked her head to the side.

"Do you ride?" she asked.

"Not unless it's got a clutch and handlebars. But I rode a couple of times as a kid. Trail horses. Nothing fancy."

"Your mother didn't ride at all?"

"Not regularly, no. She rode the trail horses on vacation. That's all I remember."

"She used to spend time on the farm here." Ellie dropped her gaze, stroking Champ's nose through the bars. "She rode with my mom a lot. I think she even went on the show circuit one summer."

For some reason, Max's chest felt tight. His mother had been gone more than twenty years now and he was used to it. She was a memory. A distant, pleasant memory. But to know she'd been here? That she'd set foot on this property and spent time riding the horses?

It was oddly emotional for him. He hadn't expected that at all.

"I'm sorry," Ellie said, and he snapped his gaze to hers. She was frowning.

"Why?" he asked, his voice hoarser than he expected it to be.

She shrugged. "You looked as if you were hurting. I didn't mean to upset you."

He didn't know why, but he reached for her hand where it rested on the bar, covering it with his own. A current of heat flashed through him. Her eyes widened for a second, but she quickly masked her reaction.

"I'm not upset. Just thinking." It wasn't the truth, but he wasn't inclined to share his sorrows with a stranger. With anyone really. And yet he wished he could for a change.

"I'm glad I didn't upset you." She cleared her throat and carefully extracted her hand. He tried not to let it bother him, though it frustrated him on some level. There was attraction here, definitely. But it was probably best not to explore it. He had a brief thought that he could seduce her and talk her into selling the farm that way. As a warrior, he was accustomed to using all his skills to attack the enemy and win the battle.

But this wasn't a war and she wasn't the enemy, even if she did frustrate him.

No, he wouldn't seduce her. He only needed to use logic and facts to get her to sell. He had a brief vision of his father on his deathbed, deciding what to leave each of his sons. What had made Dad choose Applegate Farm for him, a soldier? And why hadn't Dad told him that Mom had spent time here? Of course he'd known about it. Or maybe Dad had been so doped up on painkillers that he hadn't really thought about each bequest.

You know that's not true. There's a reason for everything Dad did. A master plan. Because that's the kind of man he was.

Yes, the kind of man who planned his own death once he'd known it was coming was not the kind of man who scattered bequests as if they were birdshot aimed at the side of a barn.

Ellie was still gazing at the horse, hands in her pockets, not saying a word. Max remembered his conversation with Knox and thought maybe now was the time to mention her mother. Especially since Ellie had mentioned her first.

"You said your mother borrowed the money from my dad—but her name's not on the paperwork. Did she retire?"

She sighed. "Momma died two years ago. If she was still here, believe me, she wouldn't have retired."

Her smile seemed forced. He wanted to reach out and smooth the corners, but he knew she wasn't going to accept that.

"I'm sorry. I shouldn't have asked." Real smooth, Einstein.

"No, it's fine. She's gone. There's no other way to say it." She sucked in a breath and rocked back on her heels. "Thanks for helping me feed. I need to get up to the house and work on some things."

"I'll walk up with you. I still have carpeting to rip out."

"Wow, that's right." She shook her head slowly. "I keep forgetting you've moved yourself into my house like the new lord of the manor."

The acid was back in her tone, but it didn't seem quite as venomous this time. He wondered why. And then he told himself it didn't matter. He wanted to sell and she didn't. They were at cross-purposes and always would be.

"You know how to get me gone, Ellie."

Her jaw worked for a second and then hardened stubbornly. "Not happening, Brannigan. Not happening."

Ellie was supposed to be balancing the books and writing checks—yeah, checks, because so many of the people she dealt with, from the feed store that mixed her grain to the farrier who shod the horses, didn't have online bill-pay options—but she was busy watching Max Brannigan carry carpet to the dumpster.

He'd stopped what he was doing and offered to help her feed, and she'd been bitchy to him in the end. She hadn't been raised that way, but then again, why should she feel a moment's remorse over snapping at him? He wanted to sell her farm, and she had to keep sight of that fact. She didn't have a lot of options here. She could stall for the next five months, but if Champ didn't win in Louisville and she couldn't sell him, she was up a creek without a paddle.

There was no other plan besides that one. Show Champ to a big win in August and sell him in order to pay off the note—or what used to be the note. If Max wanted more than her mother had borrowed... Well, she had no idea how she was going to deal with that.

Surely he was capable of some sympathy. She thought of him standing in the barn and looking lost when they talked about his mother. Then he'd touched Ellie's hand, and she'd thought she might come out of her skin. That had certainly been a surprise. Electricity had zipped along her nerve endings, firing all kinds of sizzling sensations, and she'd felt an ache of need unlike any she could ever recall before.

Which was silly because she wasn't inexperienced. She'd had sex, though not a lot of it, and she'd been pretty excited about the process at the time. Max was *not* more exciting than any other man she'd been with.

You mean all two of them, Ellie?

She blew out a breath. Yes, two of them. Two men in her life ever. The second one, Dave, had been long-term. Hell, she'd thought they would get married someday. He'd talked about it. She'd talked about it. But they never made a plan—and then Momma got sick and started behaving erratically, and Dave had given up one day. Just walked in and said he couldn't take it anymore.

Ellie didn't even tear up thinking about it. Not anymore. She'd been pissed, sure. And then she'd had her hands full with Momma and she'd realized what was important in life.

Men were not important. Or reliable. She should have known that considering her father had abandoned them when she was three, but she'd been optimistic.

Well, no more. She knew better now.

And yet she watched Max work and wondered what it might be like to run her hands over those muscles. To press her mouth to his and see if the fireworks in her belly grew bigger and better.

She turned to go back to the desk, and her gaze landed on a picture tucked into one of the built-in bookshelves. Two girls sat on top of horses, smiling into the camera as if there was nothing in this world better than what they were doing at that moment. They looked full of life and hope.

Ellie went over and picked up the picture. She knew which one was Momma, but she'd never really thought about the other one. The picture had been a fixture for so long, tucked in with others, that Ellie never noticed it. Until right then, of course. Almost as if she'd been meant to pick it out from the rest today of all days.

She had a feeling who the other girl was. She could almost see Max's eyes in this girl. She should show him the picture. She clutched it for a moment, thinking. And then she set it down on her desk and sank into the seat. She had work to do, and he was busy doing work of his own.

Was she angry that he was here? Yes, of course. But she had to admit that she wasn't really all that upset if he wanted to improve his room. One less thing for her to do.

It hit her forcefully then that Applegate Farm was no longer hers. No longer even possibly hers, which it had been so long as she paid the loan. It was his. His alone. He couldn't sell it without her permission until September, true—but he could sell it then. And he *would* sell it, and all her horses with it.

If she let him sell it now, she'd have half the money. She could start over somewhere smaller, right? Her and Champ.

Everything inside her rebelled. Her stomach sank into her toes and her heart ached. If she didn't have her family farm, what would she have? She couldn't imagine the emptiness in her life if she didn't have this connection to her past. She was a steward of her family's legacy, but what a tattered legacy it was these days.

And Max was planning to sell it. Unless she convinced him not to. Could she do that? Could she show him there were reasons to keep the farm? Or reasons to give her the time she needed to buy it from him?

Hope swirled inside her like a tiny butterfly, rising and circling. This situation was not ideal. He was here, in her home, and he was the enemy to her way of life.

But she could show him the beauty of it, couldn't she? She could make him see how special Champ was. She could spend her time educating him about saddlebreds rather than taking offense at his ignorance and looking for reasons to fight with him about the future.

For whatever reason, Colin Brannigan had given her a chance when he'd put that year into the contract, and she wasn't going to waste it. Starting right now, she was going to prove to Max that he was wrong, that there was value here if he would just look for it. His mother had loved this place at one time. She'd been happy here, according to Momma.

Max could be happy too. Why not?

Ellie put her hands on either side of her face and stared at the desk calendar with its scribblings and phone numbers around the edges. She knew nothing about Max, other than who his father was. She also knew he wasn't afraid of hard work, which had been a surprise, but maybe that could work to her advantage.

She would get him involved in the day-to-day business of the farm. If he spent time with the horses, maybe he'd get attached to them.

"Wishful thinking," she muttered.

Yeah, maybe it was. But she had no choice except to try.

CHAPTER FIVE

Max pulled up the tack strips left around the room and carried them outside. Then he went searching for a broom and dustpan. He found them in a closet outside the kitchen. When he closed the door, Ellie was standing there.

He'd heard her coming, so it wasn't a surprise. She smiled at him, which *was* a surprise.

"How's it coming?"

"Just about to sweep up. You want to see?"

"Sure." She reached into her jeans pocket and pulled out a key. "Forgot to give you this earlier."

"Thanks," he said. It was warm from her pocket as he tucked it into his jeans. He tried not to think of how it had lain against her body. "Come on and let me show you the room."

He'd moved the furniture up against one wall, which hadn't been difficult considering there was only a bed, a night table, and a dresser in the room.

Ellie stopped in the doorway, her eyebrows lifting as her gaze scanned the floor. "I had no idea. I mean, I knew there

43

was hardwood under the carpet, but I didn't know it was in such good shape. The room was carpeted before I was born."

"Looks like hand-scraped oak."

"The planks are wider than the wood in the hall and living room."

"Looks like this was probably a later addition to the main house."

She walked into the room and turned around. "Doesn't look so bad now, does it?"

"These old houses never do when you dig down to the bones."

She gave him a look. "I didn't know old houses were your thing."

He shrugged. "They aren't, but I've helped with a reno project or two. Spent a summer building homes for Habitat for Humanity."

He started to sweep up the dirt. Ellie didn't leave like he'd expected her to. Instead, she moved off to one side while he worked. Then she grabbed the dustpan and held it while he pushed the dirt into it.

"Thanks."

She stood. "No problem."

The floor looked a hundred times better than it had. He didn't know why he'd started ripping out the carpet, but he'd needed something to do, and that was the most immediate problem he could tackle.

Plus he'd been pissed that she'd put him in this room and thought it was enough to make him leave. He knew that's why she'd done it. The room was old, musty, hot, and not lived in. But he could fix that.

It was already cooler since he'd opened the vents, and the musty smell was much better now that the carpet was gone. The funny thing was, he'd stayed in worse. Hell, there had been nights when he'd had nothing but sand or rock for a bed. Navy SEALs didn't exactly rent hotel rooms when infiltrating a target.

Ellie didn't know he'd been a SEAL, of course, which was why she thought he would run at the first sign of inconvenience or discomfort. It was as laughable as it was annoying.

"So what next?" she asked, and he met her gaze, found himself looking into green eyes so pretty and pure that they made him wistful for the days before he knew how cruel the world could be.

"Needs polishing. No stripping or sanding just yet, though it should probably be done in the next few months."

She nodded, her gaze straying over the room that was already brighter now that the carpet was gone. "I haven't been in here in so long that I'd forgotten how big it was."

"What was this room used for?"

She tucked a lock of hair behind her ear. "It was a sitting room when I was little, but later it was Granny's bedroom for a few years until she couldn't go up the stairs to bathe anymore and we had to move her to a nursing home. Momma wanted to put in a bathroom, but Granny wouldn't hear of it. Said it was too much money and a waste."

"This would be a great master bedroom with an added bath."

"It would. I've always thought that—but it wasn't a priority, so it's never been done."

He took the dustpan from her, and their fingers brushed briefly. She gasped and then turned red and he wanted to chuckle. Except he was dealing with his own reaction to the contact.

"I'll open the windows tomorrow." He sounded gruff, but he couldn't help it. "Shouldn't be too difficult."

She licked her bottom lip nervously, and his entire body stiffened. Fucking hell.

"Hey, if you're feeling ambitious, you can open them all. Every window in this house has been painted shut."

"I'll take a look."

"Do you need help moving the furniture and putting the bed back together?"

"No. I'm just going to toss the mattress on the floor for the night."

She looked guilty. "It's not the most comfortable mattress, I'm afraid."

"Doesn't matter. It's still a mattress."

She blinked at him. "You say that like you sleep on floors a lot."

"Floors. Packed dirt. Sand. Rocks. Yeah, a mattress is a luxury."

Her expression was one of confusion. "Are you an extreme athlete or something?"

He laughed. Of course she'd heard of Luke's exploits. And she'd probably seen Hunter's photographs in *National Geographic* along with other nature publications. Both brothers were known for living on the edge. Max lived *over* the edge. Mired in the muck and blood and the detritus of war.

But that wasn't something the world wanted to know. It wasn't glamorous or daring. It was suicidal in a far more sinister way.

"No, I'm not. I'm a soldier, Ellie." He still had trouble thinking of himself that way since a SEAL was technically a sailor, but it's what others understood, so it was the term he used.

Her mouth dropped open just enough that he thought about kissing it closed. He wouldn't though.

"A soldier? Like in the military?"

He took the dustpan and broom and walked out of the room and back to the kitchen where he dumped the pan and stored it in the closet with the broom again. Ellie was there when he turned around, just like she had been when he'd first gone for the supplies.

Her brows were drawn low and she looked... worried. That was new.

"Not quite," he told her, because it was no use lying to her. "I was in the Navy for eight years, and then I got out and went to work as a private contractor."

That was the simple version. The more complicated version was that he'd vowed to leave the Navy after he and his men were caught in a clusterfuck of an operation and half of them died. He'd finished his time and gotten out, no matter that his commanding officer had begged him to stay.

"A private contractor? I don't understand. You said you were a soldier."

"I am. I was a SEAL, and I have a very special skill set that I hire out in the service of, uh, our nation's goals overseas."

That was the polite way of putting it. Fighting wars that needed fighting but that the US didn't want to be officially involved in—or didn't have enough regular troops to send in—was more accurate.

Ellie frowned. "You sound like the guy in that movie — the one who says he has a very special set of skills and he will find the guy who kidnapped his daughter and kill him even though he has nothing more to go on than a voice on the phone."

Max laughed. "You're talking about *Taken*. And yeah, it's something like that. Maybe not quite as dramatic though."

"Well, I have to say I'm quite shocked, Max Brannigan. Not at all what I expected you to tell me. I thought maybe you liked to jump off cliffs or rappel down waterfalls or scale skyscrapers the way your brother does."

"No, I've never seen the appeal of doing that."

"Then that means you aren't crazy. Which is a good thing."

"You don't think it's crazy to fight battles against terrorists—battles in which you might be maimed and mutilated before they kill you?"

He hadn't meant to say that—or any of it. It was more than he ever said to anyone, his brothers especially. She swallowed, and he realized he'd rattled her. He didn't like that. But it was too late to call back the words.

"Okay, I take it back. You are crazy." She scrubbed a hand over one arm as if she was chilled. "Is that why you want to sell my farm? To get out of that life?"

He could tell her yes. Maybe she'd soften a bit in her stance toward selling. But it wasn't the full truth. He *was* trying to make a change in his life. But he wasn't trying to escape what he did. Not entirely. He just wanted more control over it.

"Not precisely. I want to open my own business protecting high-level clients in—let's say *questionable*—situations around the world. Still risky, but not as much as what I do now. I need money to invest in start-up costs."

He didn't know why he was telling her that. It was more than he'd said to anyone in so long it kind of shocked him. But she loved her farm, and he wanted her to sell it. He thought she deserved to know why. And there was just something about her that made telling her these things seem natural.

She shook her head. "You're a Brannigan. Your father was worth billions. How can you possibly need to sell my farm? You must have inherited a fortune."

"I didn't. The estate is in trust for the next five years. I don't get a penny until then. None of us do."

And he simply couldn't imagine spending five more years doing contract jobs in the world's hellholes. He wanted to call his own shots, build his own business. Choose the jobs his people took.

Her mouth had dropped open. "Wow. I think I may be just a little bit pissed at your father right now. I hope you don't mind."

He had an odd urge to chuckle. "No, I'm a little pissed at him myself."

"If you'd inherited your share of the estate, you wouldn't want my farm. I could keep paying the loan off and no one would care. Hopefully."

"That's probably true."

"Couldn't you get loans against what you stand to inherit?"

"Five years is a long time, Ellie. If the world economy goes bust for some reason, who knows what could happen to the estate?"

"I doubt it would go belly-up."

"Maybe not. But I doubt a bank is going to give me money with that thought in mind."

She looked fierce. "Have you even tried? Or was selling my farm the first thing that came to mind?"

She had him there. "It's the most valuable thing I currently own. Of course it's the first thing that came to mind."

She blew out a breath. "Okay, I get that. But isn't there another way? Can't we think of something that helps me keep my farm until I can pay you back?"

"I could probably use the farm as collateral—"

"No," she said fiercely. "Please don't. If you do that, I might never get it back."

He looked at the desperation in her gaze, at the way her pulse throbbed in her neck, and felt a wave of protectiveness sweep through him. Dammit, it was part of his programming to take care of those who needed his help. Always had been, even as a kid. Especially after Mom died and the randomness of the universe struck him with its unfairness.

She'd been going to get ice cream. Because she'd wanted her boys to have a treat. She'd never come home, and he'd never stopped thinking about how he could have stopped it from happening. That had made him super protective of his brothers, even when they didn't want it. If anything risky, ever, he insisted on going first. Jumping into the lake from the top of a cliff. Lighting the fireworks on July Fourth. Racing his bike over the huge jumps they'd set up.

If anyone was going to break a bone or lose a finger, he'd been determined it was going to be him. Not that his brothers let him get away with it all the time. It was easier with the younger ones than the three eldest, but he'd tried. He'd butted heads with James often because his eldest brother had stepped into a parent role after their mother died and wouldn't be budged.

Now Max wanted to do something to protect Ellie from the fear of losing her farm. *Dammit.* Just like that, he was ready to throw himself off the cliff and into the water before anyone else.

"Then I won't do it."

She swallowed. "Just like that?"

"Just like that. I won't use the farm as collateral for a loan before September comes. I'm not promising I won't sell it then, but I *will* work to convince you that selling now is the best path for us both. All I ask is that you be honest with yourself. Look at the situation objectively."

She didn't speak for a few seconds. "I'll try."

It was more than he'd expected.

But she wasn't done. "Why didn't you come sooner? The year is up in September, and I'd have thought you'd have been here as soon as you found out."

"I was busy." Mostly that was true. He'd been too mired in work to come home and open an envelope. And after he'd heard what his brothers had gotten, he hadn't been in a hurry to find out what sort of odd bequest Dad had left him. He still didn't understand what he was supposed to do with a horse farm or how he was going to convince this woman to sell it.

Time to shift gears. "I hope you'll pardon the phrase, but I'm so hungry I could eat a horse right now. Please tell me there's pizza delivery around here."

She grinned as she reached for a stack of papers sitting on top of some cookbooks. "I have a few menus. Take a look. And while we have plenty of horses, it would take too long to cook one."

"Humor, Ellie?"

She shrugged. "I'm capable of it."

He took the menus from her hand, being careful not to touch her this time. "Care to join me, or do you have other plans?"

She dropped her gaze for a moment. "No plans. I could eat pizza."

"Excellent."

She'd told him she would try to look at the idea of selling the farm objectively, but the truth was every time she tried to imagine herself selling, she reacted violently. Her heart squeezed and her mind rebelled. Her entire body was alive with one thought: *no*.

So why had she said it? She didn't know, though maybe it was his soulful eyes or his deep voice that had made it seem reasonable to agree at the time. But she wasn't going to sell. She was going to convince him to keep the farm until she could buy it back.

The pizza came and they sat on the back porch, eating slices and gazing out at the sun setting over the bluegrass. It was so beautiful it hurt sometimes. Horses grazed peacefully, tails swishing as they moved through the pasture.

Applegate Farm wasn't just a farm to her. It was in her blood, her bones. How could she explain that to him? And yet she understood why he wanted to start his own business. Why he wanted to get away from fighting terrorists. Not that she imagined protecting CEOs was going to be a cakewalk, but it had to have fewer risks than constantly fighting battles on the front lines—and maybe he would be too busy running the operation to be the one going on assignments.

There were so many things she wanted to ask him, but she didn't know how to even begin to do so. She'd never been anywhere outside the United States. There was always work to do on the farm and horses to train. Other than traveling for shows, she didn't go anywhere.

"So you grew up here?" he asked, and she started at the unexpected sound of his voice.

"Mostly, yes."

"Mostly?"

Now why had she said that? She cleared her throat and grabbed another slice of pizza. Too late now. And truth be told, she kind of wanted to talk about it. Maybe he'd understand her better if she did.

"Momma went through a phase. We moved to Louisville for a year or so when I was seven. She had a boyfriend—it didn't work out." She took a bite of pizza and chewed. "My daddy left when I was three. I don't really remember him. We lived here with Granny and Gramps for four years, and then Momma met Stewart. He promised her grand things, but he never delivered—except for the time he took us to stay at the Seelbach Hotel in Louisville one weekend. I remember being very impressed with the grand staircase in the lobby and all the wood paneling. And then Momma told me that F. Scott Fitzgerald set some of *The Great Gatsby* there. Not that I understood what any of that meant at the time."

"Sounds impressive."

"Are you familiar with the book?"

"I saw the movie."

"I remember the ballroom on the tenth floor where Momma said that Daisy had met Gatsby. It was so pretty. When I was old enough, I read the book—and promptly despised Daisy for being weakhearted and stupid."

"Things you are not."

She warmed at the compliment. "I don't think so, no." She sighed. "Other than that trip and the Kentucky State Fair, I hated Louisville. It's a little over an hour away, so I got to come back on weekends, but I hated not living on the farm or being around the horses."

"It's peaceful here. I see why you love it."

It was peaceful. Lonely too, though she wasn't admitting that to him. It had been lonely for a long time now. It hadn't been lonely when Momma was alive and well. They'd had so many plans. Her heart ached hard at the memories of all they'd had and all they'd planned.

"Oh, I wanted to show you something," she said. "Be right back."

She went into the house and grabbed the photo she'd found and then walked back outside. He was sitting where she'd left him, sipping a bottle of water and gazing at the scenery.

"I think it's your mother."

He took the photo and stared at it for a long while. "Yeah, it is. Wow, she was so young."

"Probably about fifteen in that photo."

"Right before she met my dad. They met when she was seventeen, but they didn't get together for another ten years." He was quiet for a few moments. "So she really knew how to ride, huh? Did she do what you were doing earlier?"

Ellie sat down again. "No, she didn't ride five-gaited according to my mother. But she showed one of our three-gaited horses that summer. Won a couple of the classes and placed high in the others."

"Do you mind if I take a picture of this?"

"No, of course not."

He set the photo down and took out his phone. After he snapped a pic, he said, "I have to send this to my Aunt Claire. I think she'll love it. I'm pretty sure she doesn't have it because I think if she'd had a copy, she'd have shared it by now."

"I don't know that there were any copies made at the time. That's probably the only one there is. You're welcome to take it and have it digitized."

"Thanks. I might do that." He set the picture on the table and leaned back in his chair. "It's funny to think our mothers might have sat right here on this porch and watched the horses and now we're doing the same."

"I miss my mother," Ellie said, her heart swelling. She wanted to bite her lip. Why had she said that? Why did she say so many personal things around him? He wasn't her friend, though she didn't really think he was the enemy anymore either. An enemy actively despised you. He did not despise her. And she didn't despise him either. Not now.

"I'm sorry. People say it gets easier with time, and it does, but that's such a hollow sentiment. It never stops affecting you."

"No, it definitely doesn't." Ellie yawned and set her plate down, done with pizza and confessions for the time being. "I think I'm going to bed now. Thanks for ordering pizza."

"Thanks for sharing it with me."

Ellie started to speak but nodded instead when she realized she didn't know what more to say. Then she turned and went inside and up the stairs to her bedroom, chastising herself the whole way for sitting outside and eating pizza with him. Yes, she'd resolved to be nice and win him over to her way of thinking about the farm. But that didn't mean she needed to spend personal time with him, getting to know him and aching for him when he thanked her for showing him a picture.

Dammit!

Ellie did *not* want to like him. But she feared it was already too late.

CHAPTER SIX

Ellie didn't sleep well. She tossed and turned and dreamed about terrorists with black robes that covered them from head to toe, brandishing automatic rifles and parading captured soldiers in front of a camera before lining them up and shooting them dead.

She knew that what terrorists typically did was far worse, but her mind wouldn't go there. Thankfully.

After a restless night, she woke around five, as usual, but her heart was pounding and her eyes were as gritty as if she'd been awake all night. She told herself it was just the dreams and not the fact she'd shared pizza and conversation with Max Brannigan—and liked it.

In spite of the urge to turn over and go back to sleep, she knew that wasn't happening as she pushed herself upright. She had horses to feed and work, and they couldn't be ignored. She got out of bed and pulled on work jodhpurs, boots, and a sports bra and T-shirt before pulling her hair back into a ponytail and splashing water on her face. After she'd brushed her teeth, she went down the stairs and turned on the Keurig. The house was quiet and she crept through the kitchen, wincing at every creaking board. She didn't want to wake Max. She had no idea how late he'd stayed up, but she hadn't heard him come in.

She grabbed a mug and some cream. When she turned to put the cream back in the fridge, she gasped and jumped, nearly dropping the container.

Max stood there in a T-shirt and jeans, looking more awake than she felt at the moment. His dark hair was tousled, but his eyes were sharp.

"Sorry," he said. "I heard you and figured it was time for coffee."

She slipped her mug under the Keurig and popped in a K-cup before pressing the button. "Definitely is. And then it's time to feed horses."

"Can I help?"

Her fingers trembled as she reached for her coffee. What the hell?

Okay, so maybe it was a fantasy to find a partner who would get up early and have breakfast with her before helping with the horses, but Max was not the partner, and he wasn't fulfilling her fantasy.

Still, it fit with her plans to involve him in the running of the farm, so why not?

"Sure. I can always use the help. I'm not paying you though."

He snorted. "Didn't think you would. The labor is free."

"Because you own the place," she said and then wished she hadn't. They'd made progress last night, and here she was shooting it up with both barrels.

He shrugged as he got out his own mug and set it under the nozzle. "Well, yeah, I do. But anything I help you with benefits us both. We split the profits, remember?"

"Only for a year, which is already half up. Then you keep everything."

"Which is why you should agree to sell sooner rather than later."

He turned away to fix his coffee, and she lifted her mug and took a sip. Was there anything better than a creamy cup of coffee first thing in the morning?

Mind-blowing sex and then *coffee.*

Ellie frowned at the voice in her head. Not where she wanted her mind to go this early.

But her eyes had a different plan as they slid down Max's back, over his fine rear end, and then back up to broad shoulders. When he turned to face her again, she took another sip of coffee and hoped her cheeks weren't red.

"I'll think about it," she said. She *would* think about it. That was not a lie, even if she already knew the outcome.

Max's brows drew down and then he laughed. "Sure you will. Humoring me, Ellie?"

She shrugged. Now why did he make her insides warm up when he joked with her? "I said I'd try to be objective. Maybe I'm perfectly serious."

He snorted. "Nice try. You aren't serious. Not yet. You'll get there, but not overnight."

"You never know."

"I know," he said, taking his coffee and going over to the table. "But I appreciate that you're working at it."

Now that just made her feel guilty. She wasn't objective. Not at all. "Do you want some cereal? I have corn flakes and Cheerios."

"Sure. Cheerios sounds good."

She brought the box and milk, then retrieved bowls and spoons from the cabinet. He let her go first and then he poured his own. She didn't look at him while they ate. She hadn't had anyone at the breakfast table with her in over two years now. Miguel ate at home, and Lacey usually came out later in the morning.

"How big is this house?" Max asked as they ate.

"About four thousand square feet, I think. I close off most of the rooms in summer and winter. It's just me, so it makes no sense to heat and cool all this space. In spring and fall, I open the doors and let the house air out. I managed to get a couple of the windows open last year, one at the front and one at the back, so there's a cross breeze. I just haven't had time to work on the others."

"I'll tackle the ones in my room later. We'll see how that goes."

"Any further renovation plans for the room?"

"I'm buying a new mattress. That one sucks."

She snorted. "I thought you said it wasn't going to be problem."

"It wasn't—for a night."

"You don't need to buy one, Max. There's a guest bedroom upstairs that's not being used. You can stay there."

He grinned. "I thought you wanted me gone. And now you're letting me have a new room?" He shook his head. "Nope, not accepting. Besides, when I said I was getting a new mattress, I meant an air mattress. I like that room. I'm not giving up on it."

For some reason, that filled her with warmth. He liked the room, and he liked sitting on the porch. Yesterday morning, she'd thought he was looking down his nose at the genteel decay of her home, and now she knew that wasn't really true. Max wasn't quite what she'd thought he was.

She remembered her dreams, and the reality of what he did made a shiver slip down her spine. Her spoon clanked the bowl. It was his life. She didn't care what he did with it. She didn't know him well enough to care.

And yet...

Max was gazing at her questioningly, but he didn't say anything.

"Sorry," she said, carefully moving her spoon so it didn't clank again. "Klutzy sometimes."

"Hopefully not while riding."

It took her a moment to realize he was teasing. "Well, it happens. Not often, thankfully. I lost a rein once when I was showing in a big class. My horse stumbled and the rein slipped right out of my grip. I got it back, but it was embarrassing." Here she couldn't quite contain a laugh. "And then there was the time my saddle wasn't tight enough and the horse cut the corner sharp—and I went sliding over the side. Needless to say, I lost that class."

Max looked horrified. "That sounds dangerous."

"Really? You of all people are talking to me about danger?"

He frowned. "Well, yeah. That saddle thing sounds like a failure to inspect the equipment."

She nodded. "You bet your ass that's what it was. I thought Momma was doing it, and she thought I was doing it. Neither one of us did. That was five years ago, and it's never happened again."

"You show pretty regularly?"

Sadness churned inside her. "I used to. We had a show string—five to ten horses sometimes. And we had clients too, people who came to Momma for training, and we'd go to the shows with a load. Now it's just going to be me and Champ and a couple of clients who will show this year. We'll be making the rounds, trying to get enough points to qualify for Louisville."

The first show was coming in two weeks. She had so much riding on it. Champ needed to win his debut. And then he needed to win or make the top two in every show after that. Not for points, but for reputation and value. The more he won, the better it would be. If he got to Louisville undefeated? His worth would be unquestionable.

But they had to get through this first show, and that worried her.

"What's Louisville?"

"The World's Championship Horse Show. It's a big deal in our world. If Champ wins the three-year-old five-gaited division—well, it would be huge. And potentially very good for Applegate Farm."

"So there's money? Like a purse?"

"The biggest money is in the World's Grand Championship class on Saturday night. One hundred thousand dollars. But no, Champ won't be competing for that. Not yet. Maybe someday."

"So how would this be good for the farm?"

"Someone will want to buy him if he wins. They'll want to take him to the World's Grand Championship class someday, and they'll pay a lot of money for that opportunity."

He looked interested. "How much money?"

Ellie's heart sped up even thinking about it. "Potentially? A million or thereabouts. Depends on how good he looks and who's watching."

Max was staring at her like he'd never heard such nonsense in his life. Then he blinked and laughed. "Damn, you're telling me that fancy prancing horse out there is worth a million dollars? A prancer, not a racehorse like American Pharoah?"

Ellie frowned, but she wasn't really upset. "A prancer? Let me see you get your ass up there on his back and find out what happens. And I said potentially, by the way."

Max held up both hands. "Fine, potentially. Also, not getting on him. I know what my skills are, and riding isn't one of them."

"Champ isn't a prancer. He's a marvel. A five-gaited colt with so much talent he can set the world on fire if he gets the chance. Horses like that come around once in a lifetime. We'll probably never have another Wing Commander or Skywatch, but one day people will say we'll never have another Applegate's No Regrets either."

"Don't take this the wrong way, Ellie—but how's Champ going to save the farm for you if the farm already owns him? That money is technically the farm's, right? Not yours?"

She didn't blame him for asking the question, because it *was* confusing. "I own Champ. Momma gave him to me for a birthday present because she knew I loved him at first sight. We've always personally owned some of the horses while the others belong to the farm. Kind of an insurance policy, I guess."

His smile was genuine. "That's good. I like knowing he's yours no matter what. And now I guess we've got work to do, huh?"

Max pushed his bowl back and drained his coffee. Ellie tried not to stare at his backside as he got up and went to the sink to wash—holy cow, *wash*—his own dishes. But it was a mighty fine backside, and it looked pretty darn good encased in faded jeans. And then there was the part where he seemed genuinely happy that Champ was hers. How could she not like him, in spite of the fact he wanted to talk her into selling her farm?

She finished her cereal and stood, but Max was there before she could get to the sink, taking the bowl from her and washing it before stacking it in the rack to dry.

Ellie downed her coffee and Max took her cup. "Thank you."

His gray eyes were warm, and they made her pulse flutter. "You're welcome."

Her eyes stung for no good reason as he walked away. She smoothed her hands over her hair, ostensibly making sure her ponytail was tight, but mostly because she needed something to do.

"Ready?" Max asked as he turned around again.

"Sure. Let's go feed horses."

He shook his head.

"What?"

"If you'd told me a week ago I'd be toting hay to horses, I'd have said you were crazy."

"What were you doing a week ago?" she asked as they stepped onto the back porch and started for the barn.

"You don't want to know, Ellie."

No, she probably didn't.

Max hadn't meant to get up so early, but some habits were hard to break. The truth was he didn't need a lot of sleep. In fact, he was used to sleeping in short snatches downrange. You never went fully to sleep while in a foxhole. You cat-napped, grabbing sleep whenever you could.

If he ever slept a whole night through again, he'd be completely surprised. He'd spent too many years doing it that way to ever change. Of course he slept in two- and three-hour increments when not fighting, but he still woke regularly and he still prowled through the darkness when he did. Last night he'd gone back outside and sat on the porch, listening to the night sounds until he was tired enough—or calm enough, he wasn't sure which—to sleep again.

Ellie walked beside him, her strides shorter than his but no less determined. Still, he paced himself to her stride. The sun wasn't above the horizon yet, but the sky was already purple and orange. The grass was wet with dew, and birds chirped in the morning air. It was cool but not chilly. The barn lay ahead like a white beacon. There was a cupola on the top of the barn and a weather vane. It would make a pretty picture.

He nearly came to a full stop, wondering where the hell that thought had come from. He did not think in terms of pretty pictures or perfect Kentucky mornings, yet here he was, thinking both things.

He shook his head. Ellie had asked him where he was a week ago. He hadn't told her because he'd been deep behind enemy lines, striking a terrorist training camp and capturing one of their most feared leaders before obliterating the camp and ruining their ability to train. It had been ugly, as such things always were. There were casualties. One of them had been a former Green Beret he'd worked with on a couple of ops in the past year.

Max hadn't known Robert well, but there was something about his death that had pushed Max to seriously start thinking about his idea to open a personal-security company of his own. It would still be dangerous, but not as much so. Not as totally random as what he did now.

They walked past the field where a group of horses nickered to them. Ellie went over and petted noses. Max noticed that one of the horses was fat. Seriously fat.

"Is that horse pregnant?"

Ellie turned, a smile on her face. "Yes. She's due this month. We'll bring her in soon so she can foal in the barn."

"And the others?"

"I only bred four last year, so this is the last baby to come. All right, ladies, let me get moving. Miguel will be here shortly with your feed."

They started down the path again. When they reached the barn, a short man with dark hair was already there, loading hay into a John Deere Gator. He stopped when they approached, his face breaking into a broad smile.

"Good morning, Ellie," he said, his voice rich with hints of his native Spanish.

"Morning, Miguel. This is Max Brannigan," she said, waving a hand at Max. "He's an old friend of the family, and he's staying for a few days. He wants to help out."

Max nearly swallowed his tongue at the smoothness of Ellie's lie. But he went with the flow, holding out his hand and shaking Miguel's. The other man's hands were strong, and he wasn't afraid to give a firm handshake. Max liked that.

"You'll have to go easy on me," Max said to him. "I don't know much about horses."

"He doesn't know anything, Miguel," Ellie said with a smile. "Thinks we have fancy prancers around here."

Miguel let out a whoop and slapped his leg. "Prancers. That's right, *amigo*. They prance and snort and do the prettiest dance around the ring you ever did see."

"He came when I was working Champ yesterday."

Miguel nodded appreciatively. "You are lucky, Max. That horse is special. He be a big champion someday."

"We hope," Ellie said, but she was still smiling.

"Okay, I get down to the broodmare pasture now." Miguel swung up into the Gator and popped it into gear. It roared down the hill toward the pasture, and Miguel waved.

"Seems like a nice guy," Max said.

"He is. He's been with us for a decade. We used to have more help, but we had to let them go one by one. I keep Miguel because he's as much a part of the farm as I am. And because I can't do it without him."

"He doesn't know about the loan?"

The corners of her mouth tightened. "He knows. He doesn't know *who* Momma borrowed the money from. I said you were an old family friend because your father was, in a way. I'll tell him soon, but I didn't think now was the time."

"I'm not upset about it."

She gazed at him, her green eyes so serious and sad, and he felt the jolt of that look down to his core.

"Thank you."

"I'm not trying to make life hard for you, Ellie. I'm not an asshole."

"I know."

It was just about the nicest thing she could have said to him.

"What about Lacey?" he asked.

"She's not an employee. She's a friend, and she keeps her horse here. She also helps me around the barn a lot. I'll tell her because otherwise she's going to wonder why you've parked yourself in my house. She already knows you aren't an old friend because she was here when you arrived and I didn't know you, so that angle won't work with her."

"You thought I was the HVAC guy."

Her eyes widened. "Oh damn, I need to check on that! I completely forgot, and Roger didn't call me with a time for today."

"Is there a problem?"

"No, it's just a regular service. It's an old system and I'm a little paranoid about it, so I make sure to get it checked every spring and fall."

"Sounds like a good plan." It was, but it bothered him that she worried about so many things. She closed off rooms to keep her bills down, worked her ass off to take care of all these horses, and nursed her old HVAC along because she likely didn't have the money to fix it if it broke. How she'd kept this place going, especially after her mother died, was a mystery to him.

He needed to see the books. He had a right to ask, but he

almost hated to do it. She wasn't going to be happy, and that would put a dark cloud over any progress they'd made. Not that he should care since he wasn't here to make friends, but oddly enough, he did.

Still, he had to see what was going on, and looking at the books was the only way. He decided he wouldn't ask about it just now, however. The day was long, and there was plenty of time to do so. First, he wanted to see how much work there was on a day-to-day basis. He believed in getting to know a situation from the bottom up. It was the only way to truly know what he had and what needed to be done. When he was finished, he'd understand everything about how this farm worked, even if he didn't know much about horses.

Except he planned to learn that too, or as much as he could. He might not ride them, but he could read up on saddlebreds and see what the big deal was.

Ellie flipped on the barn lights and then went and loaded up the wheelbarrow. Max got the hay. He knew what to do today, so he followed along and tossed hay into each stall. When he opened Champ's stall, the big horse swung his head over to look even though he didn't stop munching his grain. He was a beautiful animal, sleek and shiny, his coat a deep red that rippled with muscle. Max couldn't imagine climbing up on that horse and making him do anything.

He closed the stall and went down the line until everyone had hay. Ellie put up the wheelbarrow and grabbed the hose, walking down the aisle and watering every horse. Hell, all they'd done was feed, and it was already a lot of work.

"You do this twice a day?"

"Yes," she said. "There's more too. Once a week, we

strip all the buckets out of the stalls and clean them. That takes time. Later, we'll pick out the stalls. Miguel mucks them out every week, and we put in clean shavings. That takes several hours with the two of us. Lacey helps as she can, but she has her own work to do."

"And then there's maintenance on the equipment, the ordering of supplies, and the horse training," he said.

"Yes. And don't forget harvesting hay. That's time consuming, plus we have to find help to bring it in or risk losing it in the field if the weather turns. During show weeks, Miguel has to do everything. Momma and I used to take a couple of our grooms with us, but now it'll just be me when I go on the show circuit. Miguel has to stay behind and take care of the farm. Lacey goes when she can." She shrugged. "It's just the way it is now."

She baffled him and amazed him. "How do you keep all the balls in the air, Ellie?"

"Very, *very* carefully."

CHAPTER SEVEN

It was going to be a long day on the farm, but most days were. Ellie gave two lessons to students and then lunged a couple of the horses before Lacey arrived around nine thirty. Her friend climbed from her car, her blond hair pulled back in a ponytail and her smile as wide and friendly as ever. Ellie's heart pinched tight as she thought of Lacey's sweetness being abused by Brice Parker. But Brice wasn't in the picture anymore, thank God. He'd finally done something unforgivable, and Lacey had dumped him. If only he'd stop harassing her, life would be perfect.

Lacey reached into her car and retrieved two cups of coffee. Ellie accepted one with a grin when Lacey walked over.

"You know me so well."

"I do. I know you haven't been back up to the house yet to get another cup. I also know there's a dumpster beside the house, and Max Brannigan's truck is parked up there. Did you hire a contractor?"

Oh, if only it were that simple. Ellie sipped her coffee and dreaded telling Lacey the truth. But Lacey was her oldest friend. If she couldn't confide in Lacey, who could she confide in?

"It's not quite that easy to explain," she began. She only hesitated once or twice, but she told Lacey all about the loan and the fact Max Brannigan now owned Applegate Farm—and apparently wanted to sell it so he could start his own business.

Lacey looked a little shell-shocked. And then she launched into crisis mode, which was one of the things Ellie loved most about her. If Lacey came up against a situation she couldn't control, she went about figuring out how to fix it and take back as much control as she could get. Other than the situation with Brice, she usually succeeded.

"But you have until September, so that's good. Champ will win at Louisville, someone will pay ridiculous money for him, and you can write Max a check. In the meantime, you get some free labor."

"What if Champ doesn't win? I don't want to sell him at a loss." Ellie frowned. "I don't want to sell him at all—but what choice do I have? He's the only way I can keep the farm. I'll never be able to afford to breed anything to him once he's gone though."

"Which is why you have a couple of his babies on the ground now. Maybe one of them will follow in his footsteps."

It was always possible, which was why Ellie had very carefully chosen the mares and bred them to him. One of the four might have that element of greatness. Or they might not, but if Champ won at Louisville, their prices would go up immediately. They were currently his only babies on the ground, which would make them desirable.

"And the point is," Lacey continued, "you have some time here. Max can't sell the farm yet. So don't panic."

Ellie sipped the coffee. "I'm not panicked. Yet."

Except for the fact he was in her house, and he was a little too pleasant to look at. No, nothing whatsoever to panic about. Just because her belly tightened and her libido sat up and took notice whenever he was near didn't mean she needed to panic. She was temporarily celibate, not dead.

The man in question emerged from the barn just then and wiped an arm across his face. He'd agreed to help Miguel muck out stalls today. She wasn't sure why, but he had. She thought maybe he was the kind of man who needed to be busy, or maybe he wanted to know more about how the farm worked before he sold it. He'd removed his shirt, which was definitely not good for her libido.

Or Lacey's, it seemed. "Oh my," she said. "Holy crap."

"Yeah, right?"

"And he's staying in your house? Like that? Girl, you need to change the plan."

"What plan? I don't exactly have a plan."

Lacey swatted at her arm, but she didn't take her eyes off Max. He hadn't yet looked over as he twisted the cap off a bottle of water and took a drink.

"The plan to sell Champ and buy the farm. Get him to stay. Permanently."

Ellie nearly choked on the coffee. "What? Why?"

"Look at him. Why not? You're twenty-eight, and your clock's ticking. You could do worse than a billionaire's son. A lot worse, trust me."

"Lacey, the fumes at the salon have gone to your head. My clock is *not* ticking. And he may be pretty, but if he turns out to be an asshole then he's not worth the trouble. Need I remind you about Dave? Or that crazy ex of yours?"

She'd told Max she knew he wasn't an asshole, but what if she was wrong? What if, when push came to shove, he really was a jerk? Wouldn't be the first time she'd gotten it wrong.

Lacey gave her a look. "Seriously? The man ripped out your carpeting, and now he's mucking stalls. Is that what assholes do? Trust me, Brice only cares about himself. He would never offer to help unless it benefited him somehow."

Ellie's cheeks flamed. Dang it. "Maybe. Look, Max owns the place. Technically. So maybe he feels obligated to keep his property in fine order. I don't know—but mucking stalls does not automatically exclude him from assholeland down the road. Dave mucked stalls."

"He worked here at the time. Doesn't count."

Ellie frowned at her. "Go get your horse and stop wasting my time."

Lacey grinned over her shoulder as she walked away. "I'm just saying, Ellie. Might at least be worth taking for a spin."

U

It turned out that mucking stalls was seriously hard work. Miguel showed Max how to dig up the wet spots and old shavings and then toss them into the wagon attached to the tractor that sat in the aisle. Once they'd gone down the row of stalls, they had to get fresh shavings for each stall and shovel them in. It was backbreaking, sweaty work. It was also smelly.

But Max didn't shrink from it. God knew he'd suffered through worse. Carrying a buddy six miles to the extraction point, weighed down with weapons and feeling his blood seeping into your clothing, was a lot worse than horse piss.

"It's good Ellie have a friend," Miguel said at one point. "She no have many people who can help her."

Max couldn't stop himself from asking, "She doesn't have a boyfriend?"

Miguel smiled a crafty smile. Okay, so asking that question wasn't precisely subtle.

"No, nobody since Dave. He used to do work here when Miss Pamela had a full barn. There was much more to be done then. Dave left when Miss Pamela got sick. It was no surprise after what happened—but what he do to Ellie was wrong."

There was a lot to process in that statement. Max stopped shoveling shavings and frowned. "What happened to Ellie's mother?"

Miguel looked fierce, and then he just looked sad. "She got a brain tumor. She was sick for a while, acted crazy sometimes and not crazy others. Did terrible things and most of the clients left. When she finally learn what was wrong, it was too late to fix anything."

Max wondered if he meant the brain tumor or the situation with the clients and decided he actually meant both.

"When the clients left, we had to let people go. That is why Dave left. But he break up with Ellie too?" Miguel shook his head. "She never complain, but I know it hurt her."

Max hated the idea of Ellie being hurt, but he couldn't say he wasn't unhappy that she didn't have a current boy-friend. Though the idea of Ellie being single for the past two years or more was rather surprising. She was a lovely wom-an. It was hard to imagine there hadn't been other men, other dates.

"It hasn't been easy for Ellie, has it?"

"No. She been building up the client list again, slowly, but they are not the same kind of people we have before." Miguel leaned forward conspiratorially. "If you ask me, I like these people better. They are not rich, they do not pur-chase expensive horses and complain if their child no win the blue every time. They are hardworking, love the animals, and don't expect Ellie to perform miracles. Miss Pamela put up with a lot of shit from people, so it was no wonder she lost control of her tongue when the tumor grew. It would have been better if she had not, but we cannot cry over spilled milk."

No, you shouldn't dwell on the past, but sometimes that was easier said than done. Max liked that Miguel was so straightforward and honest. He was a good man to have on your side, and Max was glad Ellie had him.

"You know," Max began, because he couldn't see keep-ing the truth from this man any longer when he'd been so kind, "Ellie wasn't sure how to tell you this, but I'm actually the son of the man who made the loan on the farm. I own it now."

Miguel didn't look surprised. "I know the name Branni-gan. Ellie no think I do, but Miss Pamela tell me. So yes, I know you aren't here as a friend."

"I don't mean her harm," Max said.

Miguel shrugged, but it wasn't an unconcerned shrug. More of a *what can anyone do* kind of shrug. "I hope not, *amigo*. Ellie deserve happiness for a change."

They continued working on the stalls for another hour. Ellie came and went inside the barn. A couple of kids arrived with their mothers. They saddled horses and went outside to ride. He could hear Ellie instructing them. He didn't understand what a lot of it meant—soft hands, easy, inside leg, more snaffle—but the tone of her voice was firm and yet encouraging at the same time. She exuded confidence in what she was doing.

He thought of her on the porch last night, sounding so small and lost when she'd said she missed her mother. He'd wanted to reach out and take her in his arms. It was as much a surprise to him as it would have been to her if he'd done it. But she'd gotten up and said she was going to bed, and that was the end of that.

He glimpsed that hint of vulnerability in her from time to time, and it intrigued him precisely because she did seem so strong and in control. He wondered what it would be like to make her lose that control. What it would be like to see her spread out on his bed, her hair wild and free, her lithe body bared for his delight before he took her over the edge.

He shook his head to rid it of that image. He didn't need to get involved, didn't need to take what was essentially a business relationship across the line into personal territory. How much harder would that make it for him to sell this place when time was up? Or to convince her to sell before then?

He knew himself. He liked women and he liked sex, but that's all it would be. He didn't do relationships. Didn't

77

commit. Ellie didn't need that in her life, not after what Miguel had said about Dave. She needed someone she could rely on, not someone who might jet off at a moment's notice to a foreign location where he'd be putting his life on the line. She didn't need someone who might not come back.

She needed stability, not instability. As much as he might like to kiss her senseless and explore her lovely body, he wasn't going to cross that line. They could be friends, maybe, but that was it. And even that wasn't necessary since once the farm was gone, they'd never need to see each other again.

Ellie headed up to the house around twelve thirty and found Max hard at work in his room. She could hear the sounds of scraping and sanding, so she went down the hallway to the former sitting room. Max had his back to her. He was wearing a T-shirt, thankfully, and jeans. The way the shirt stretched across his shoulders had her thinking about what Lacey said earlier. *Might at least be worth taking for a spin.*

As if her body wanted to chime in on that possibility, her nipples tightened and her core started to ache. *Jeez.*

She cleared her throat to let him know he wasn't alone. He stopped scraping off the peeling plaster and turned with a warm grin. He was covered in plaster dust. "I already knew you were standing there. Figured I'd let you ogle my ass for a while first."

Heat rolled through her. "I was *not* ogling your ass."

"Then why did you wait before announcing your presence?"

He had her there. She folded her arms over her breasts and leaned against the doorjamb. "I didn't want to scare you. I was being polite."

He snorted. "If that's what you call it."

"It is." Because there was no use arguing with him. She'd only turn redder, and she'd lose by default.

"What's up?" he asked, setting the scraper down and picking up a bottle of water.

"I heard the noise in here. I wondered what you were doing."

He gestured to the wall. "I decided to scrape off the chipping plaster and peeling paint before patching and sanding the wall. I can paint it if you decide on a color. No gloss or semigloss though. They'll show too many of the imperfections in the plaster."

Ellie walked into the room and turned around in it. Granny had picked the yellow because she wanted something sunny, but Ellie didn't like it. Never had, and neither had Momma. "Honestly, I know it might be crazy, but I want something creamy. Not quite white. Something that contrasts with the moldings but isn't so bright as this yellow. Something that suits a home of this age."

"Maybe we could run to the paint store and look at samples at some point."

"That would be great."

He set the water down and picked up a towel, wiping it across his forehead and dropping it on the mattress again. "Never thought I'd be working my ass off when I set out for this place two days ago."

"Life is full of surprises," she said. "I never thought I'd have a roommate either. Yet here we are."

"Here we are."

She hated feeling nervous around him, and yet she did. It was Lacey's fault, dammit. She'd set up the idea that Ellie should give in to her attraction to this man in spite of the fact he held a metaphorical ax over her head.

Liar. You already had that idea.

"Thanks for helping Miguel today."

"It wasn't a problem."

"It's hard work. And smelly. A lot of people don't appreciate that."

He laughed. "Ellie, compared to what I usually do, this is a walk in the park. Trust me, there's nothing I've done yet that makes me want to run screaming. I suppose that disappoints you, but the truth is I'm actually enjoying myself. It's hard work, backbreaking work—but nobody's trying to kill me."

Her heart squeezed at the thought of him in danger. She did not understand why he did what he did. He came from the kind of family where he had so many options in life. But how could she judge? She could have done something besides work with horses too, but that was her choice. She'd never wanted to do anything else, even when Momma had encouraged her to do something that would give her more security and stability.

So he was an adrenaline junkie like some of his brothers. He just chose to add in the element of having people shoot at him.

"Well," she said, trying to keep her voice light, "the horses might try to kick you or bite you, so that's an element of danger."

"You got me there. I think I can handle that though."

"I'm going to go get lunch with Lacey in a few minutes. She's cooling her horse—do you want to come with us?"

She hadn't meant to invite him. Not because it wasn't polite or she didn't want him around, but because ever since Lacey said what she did, Ellie was overthinking everything *she* said and did. Would he think she was crushing on him if she invited him to lunch? He'd already accused her of looking at his ass—which, yes, she had been—so did she need to add in more evidence that she might be attracted to him?

But how could she thank him for helping out today and then tell him she was going to lunch without asking him to go? It would be rude, right?

He hesitated for a moment, and she started mentally kicking herself. Because he surely *was* thinking that she liked him, and he was clearly not interested in return. But then he smiled at her, and her heart kicked up higher.

"Sure, I'll go. Thanks for asking. But do you mind if I meet you there? I need to take a quick shower. Then I want to get a few things afterward, so I'm going to need my truck."

Why were her insides glowing? Why was she feeling as giddy as a kid in a candy store?

Oh my God, Lacey, I am going to kill *you.*

"No rush. We aren't leaving for a while yet, so just come on down to the barn when you're ready and you can follow us there."

CHAPTER EIGHT

They took him to a restaurant in Versailles—Ver-*Sales,* they pronounced it—called Mary Lou's, a greasy spoon that turned out to have the best hamburger Max had ever had in his life. The fries were crispy and hot, and the company was far prettier than he'd been keeping in the weeks before he came to Kentucky.

He was enjoying himself, but at the back of his mind a voice whispered, *Don't go soft. This isn't your life.*

Lacey was the chattier of the two women. But Ellie chimed in here and there while Lacey talked and gesticulated wildly as she told a story. They talked about horses and about growing up together. He imagined his mother with Ellie's mom and wondered if they'd been like this. Two friends who had wild adventures together and finished each other's sentences sometimes.

He definitely needed to call Aunt Claire and ask about her and Mom's life here. He'd texted her the picture of Mom on horseback, and she'd replied with a long, gushy text that must have taken her forever to type out with just one finger—which was the way he'd seen her reply to texts in the past, picking each letter carefully—about how wonderful it was and how much Mom had loved to ride, how she'd wanted her own saddlebred but their parents couldn't afford the expense, so she'd done something called catch riding, which was basically showing someone else's horse for them. The horse she'd shown had belonged to the Applegates of course. And then Aunt Claire said she hoped he was having fun and ended by sending her love.

Max leaned back in the booth, an arm along the edge, and idly ate fries as they argued over who forgot to latch the gate on the goat pen when there used to be goats at the farm. Apparently the goats had gotten out and tap-danced all over the cars parked by the barn that day. One poor woman in a Mercedes had actually screamed and chased one of the goats down the hill before she tripped and landed in a pile of horse shit.

"Momma was so mad," Ellie said between giggles.

"Mrs. Oakley. She threatened to sue, but her husband came out the next day and apologized," Lacey said.

"Seriously?" Max asked. He could understand why Mrs. Oakley would be angry.

"Yeah," Ellie said. "There was no damage to the car, thankfully, but she said some very rude things about how important she was and how her husband would get every penny we had. He was a lawyer."

"So what happened after that?"

Ellie and Lacey exchanged a look. "Nothing. Mrs. Oakley pretended it never happened because her daughter loved riding with Momma and insisted she wasn't going anywhere else. Though Mrs. Oakley bought an SUV and drove that to the farm from then on. Lacey and I... Well, we were sixteen and we felt the loss of our privileges keenly. Momma didn't let either of us ride for two weeks."

Lacey ate a fry. "We both missed the next show. My parents were completely on board with whatever Ms. Applegate wanted to do."

"We never forgot to latch the goat pen again," Ellie said.

"Nope, never did. And then she sold the goats to a lady who wanted to make cheese, and that was the end of that."

It sounded like a fun childhood. He'd had a good childhood, even fun sometimes. Things had been difficult after his mother died and his father basically threw himself into work and disappeared, but Max and his brothers never wanted for material goods or things to do. He knew they were privileged. He knew they'd had it good even if they'd lost their mother and hardly ever did anything with their father. It was wrong to feel as if he'd missed out on anything.

But he still sometimes did.

"So what about you, Max?" Lacey asked. "What was it like growing up in California? Did you meet lots of movie stars?"

"I met a few. My father was a movie producer, so he sometimes had parties at our house."

"Who was the most memorable movie star you ever met?"

Before he could answer, Lacey's gaze flicked to the front of the restaurant and she paled. Beside her, Ellie's expression grew fierce. She reached over and squeezed Lacey's arm, and Max's danger signals went through the roof. He had his back to the door, which he did not like, but he'd told himself when he followed the ladies into the restaurant and they took a seat where he'd prefer to be sitting that he didn't need to make them move so he could face the door. He could handle himself well enough here, which was part of the reason he'd leaned into the corner of the booth so he could scan as much of the restaurant as possible from his vantage point.

Now he turned his head to see what the trouble was. He had to fight his instincts to leap to his feet and prepare to fight. Logic told him that if a gunman had walked into the restaurant, not only would Lacey and Ellie react differently, but everyone else would also be reacting—and the noise level would have changed drastically.

"It's okay," Ellie said to Lacey, who looked apprehensive. Max didn't like how the sunny Lacey had changed so suddenly. That spoke volumes.

"I know."

"He's not going to hurt you ever again."

Hurt? What the fuck?

An angry-looking man in a suit and tie swaggered through the restaurant, making a straight line for their booth. Max sized him up quickly. A big man, but a soft one. He worked out some, but he wasn't hard. He had a gut, though not much of one. His forearms were beefy, and his neck looked like he'd been a football player at one time.

He didn't appear to be armed, but you could never be 100 percent sure about that until you patted someone down.

Max got to his feet instinctively, to defend his ground and the women should it be necessary, and the man's attention landed on him. He puffed up even more as he approached, his face growing angrier.

"Brice Parker, we don't want any trouble in here," the heavyset woman at the counter called out.

"I'm not bringing any trouble," he said over his shoulder. "Just come to see my girl."

"I'm not your girl anymore, Brice," Lacey said, her face red and her eyes angry. Except she was trembling, and Max didn't like that at all. "I ceased being your girl when you cheated on me."

Max stepped into the man's path before he reached the booth. Brice kept on going, trying to bulldoze Max to the floor, but Max threw his weight forward and Brice bounced off.

"Don't make me kick your ass," Brice said. "All I want is a couple of minutes with Lacey."

"Go away, Brice," Ellie growled. "Lacey doesn't need your empty apologies."

"No, I definitely don't."

Max shrugged. "I think maybe Lacey doesn't want to talk to you, man."

Brice puffed up like a rooster as he gave Max a sneering look, his gaze sliding up and down disdainfully. "You going out with this piece of shit, Lace? Is that why you keep ignoring my calls? You got a taste for laborers now or what?"

Max didn't let things like that bother him, but he could see that Lacey had shrunk in on herself, as if she was afraid of what else this asshole might say. Or do.

"You need to get back in your BMW and head down the road," Ellie said.

"You need to shut up and stay out of this," Brice sneered. "If not for you, Lacey wouldn't be getting ideas into her head about me. You're nothing but trash, and everyone knows it." He sniffed the air. "You smell like horse shit."

Max growled. It was time to put an end to this. "Don't talk to Ellie that way. In fact, don't talk to her or Lacey *at all.*"

"Says who?"

"Me, asshole."

"Oh yeah? You big enough to stop me?"

Max snorted. "You have no idea."

Brice reared back like he was going to throw a punch, and Max rolled almost casually into action. It was easy enough to step into the man's space, grab him, and flip him around with his arm wrenched high.

Brice arched backward, whining but still defiant. "I'll fucking sue your ass!"

Max started marching him toward the door. Chairs scraped as people got out of the way. Someone opened the door and Max shoved Brice outside. He didn't let him go, however. He walked him onto the sidewalk and then pushed his face close to the man's ear.

"Sue me, asshole. I am your worst fucking nightmare. You get close to Lacey again—or Ellie—and I'll make sure they never find the pieces of what's left of your body. You got that?"

Brice stank like sweat and fear. He was nothing more than a small man in a bully's body, and he was used to getting his way. He would not get his way with Max around. Max welcomed the fierceness, the wild part of himself that could never be tamed, the part that got off on violence and adrenaline. There was a reason for that part of him to exist, and right now that reason was to protect those two women in the restaurant.

"I'll sue—" Brice's words cut off as Max twisted his arm higher, driving it upward painfully.

"Go ahead. The name's Max Brannigan. Staying at Ellie's place right now, so you can find me there when you've got your papers to serve. You feel like tangling with me, I'm ready."

He shoved hard, and Brice went stumbling onto the sidewalk. He didn't quite stay upright, however. His arms sprawled in front of him as he went down on the concrete. And then he picked himself up without looking back, scrambling upright as he ran down the street and yanked on the handle of a black BMW.

Max waited until Brice peeled out of the parking slot before he turned around and headed back into the restaurant.

Twenty people started clapping as he walked in. They were on all their feet, looking outside. Ellie and Lacey were by the counter. They'd been watching the street. Watching him. It occurred to him that he didn't know if they'd be pissed at him or what. Not that he would change what he'd done. Brice Parker was a jerk who needed his ass handed to him. If this hadn't been downtown Versailles, Kentucky— and therefore a reasonably civilized place—Max would have made sure the man never crossed him again.

Lacey's smile covered her whole face at that moment. Ellie's eyes sparkled as Lacey threw herself at him and hugged him hard for one quick second before she stepped back again.

"Thank you, Max," she said. "You didn't have to do that."

"Yeah, I did."

"Honey, that was mighty fine of you," the big woman behind the counter interrupted. She cocked her head to the side as she studied him. "I been thinking about this since you came in—you're a Hayes, aren't you? Look just like one of the Hayes girls what used to live here. Good girls they were. And Pammie," she added, smiling at Ellie. "Thick as thieves Kathy Hayes and Pammie Applegate were."

There was a knot in Max's throat. "Kathleen Hayes was my mother, yes. I'm Max Brannigan."

The woman's eyes glistened. "I'm Mary Lou," she said. "It's a pleasure to meet you, Max. A pleasure."

"Thank you, ma'am. You too."

"I was sorry to hear about your momma," she said. "Everyone in Versailles was."

"Thank you."

"Well," Ellie said brightly, "let me pay you so we can be on our way."

Mary Lou held up her hand before Max could begin to insist he was buying. "No, honey. It's on me today. Y'all enjoy your afternoon—and don't let that rotten Brice spoil your day, Lacey-bell. He's mean as a rattlesnake because his momma didn't cuddle him enough. Not your problem."

Lacey's smile shook at the corners. "I know, Mrs. Fuller."

Mary Lou patted her arm. "You go on home and don't worry about Brice. He'll think twice before bothering you again."

They left the restaurant and stepped onto the street. Out of habit, Max surveyed their surroundings. Mary Lou might think Brice wasn't coming back, but Max's training wouldn't let him assume that was the case.

"I'll walk you to your car," he said to Ellie. She didn't argue with him, and the three of them headed down the sidewalk for the small parking lot where they'd left Lacey's vehicle. It was a bright red Honda, which didn't help her stay off of Brice's radar at all. Max had half a mind to drive them back to the farm in his truck, but he knew they weren't going to accept that.

"Thanks again," Lacey said as she hit the button to open her doors. "I'm sorry you had to get involved, but so thankful you did."

"It's not a problem, Lacey."

She ducked her head as if she was embarrassed, and Ellie smiled softly. He liked that smile. She looked pleased with him. He shouldn't care, but he did.

"Guess I'll see you later," she said.

Oh yeah, the mattress he was supposed to go get. "Not a chance," he told her. "I'm following you both back to the farm."

Her eyes widened. "That's not really necessary. Brice won't go to the farm. Not since Miguel ran him off with a shotgun a couple of months ago."

Max wanted to laugh. He already knew he liked Miguel. He liked him even more now. "Still, I'll see you both home."

She quirked an eyebrow. "You planning to spend another night on that saggy mattress?"

"Only if you don't offer me a better alternative."

A better alternative? What the heck did that mean?

Ellie thought about it all the way back to the farm. She could see Max's gray truck every time she looked into the side mirror, and a current of jagged heat sizzled into her as she thought of him on the sidewalk with Brice Parker's arm shoved up between his shoulder blades.

Oh my God, the way Max had flipped Brice around and immobilized him. It would be imprinted on her memory forever. She'd actually been worried that Brice would throw a punch—but he'd never gotten the chance. Max had turned the situation around as if it was so simple to do.

Lacey had both hands on the wheel, gripping it tightly. She chattered about lunch, about Max, about anything but Brice.

Finally, Ellie couldn't take it. She put her hand on Lacey's arm and squeezed. "It's okay, Lacey. You can be upset about what happened."

Lacey shuddered and glanced at her. The stark fear on her face worried Ellie. "I know I can."

"There's something more, isn't there?" Ellie asked. "Has he done something? Are you keeping something from me?"

Lacey's face was pale. "He calls me. He leaves messages." Her fingers tightened on the wheel. "He says he won't let me go. That I have to come back."

Ellie's gut twisted. "He's an abusive jerk, Lacey. He thinks because he's a big shot business owner, he can get away with that shit. But he can't. You need to take those messages and file for a restraining order."

Lacey made a noise. "You know how he twists things. You know that none of those messages will induce a judge to

91

grant a restraining order, especially since Brice donates heavily to the police fund-raisers. He knows how to manipulate things. He'll spin it into being heartbroken and begging for forgiveness—and he'll turn today into something else too, no matter that there were witnesses. He never actually threatened me. Max acted first, even if Brice tried to throw a punch. Et cetera. He's a financial wizard, and I'm just a hairstylist and a gold digger—you know the drill."

Ellie's heart sank as she thought about it. Lacey was right that Brice would say those things. But Brice was a bully, and anyone who knew him knew that was true. Always had been. He wasn't going to win this one. Ellie wouldn't let him.

"You're staying with me tonight. No arguments."

Lacey glanced at her. "I can't do that."

"You can. You are. No arguments. I'll loan you clothing. Or we can stop by your place later."

Lacey sighed. "I don't think Max would approve of us going by my place, would he?"

Warmth spread inside her. They weren't alone in dealing with Brice. Not this time. And while she didn't ordinarily let a man tell her what to do, she figured he would be right to disapprove of a plan to make a run to Lacey's.

"Probably right. So you'll borrow some clothing. We'll have a slumber party."

Lacey smiled, and Ellie's heart hitched. She loved her friend and didn't want her hurt.

"Okay," Lacey said. "We'll pretend we're sixteen again. We'll paint each other's nails and giggle about Max."

Ellie snorted. "No nails. And no giggling."

Lacey shot her a look. "Okay, no nails. But we are totally giggling."

Ellie glanced into the mirror again. Max's truck was right there behind them. Yeah, there would be giggling all right. Because she was totally infatuated with the man who wanted to sell her farm. There was no denying it. He was tough and kind and gorgeous. Enigmatic. He intrigued her and infuriated her, and she wanted to know more.

It wasn't safe for her, emotionally, to know more. She knew that. But it didn't stop her from wanting to. He'd been in her life for a sum total of twenty-four hours, and she couldn't stop thinking about him. But was that a bad thing? He was single and gorgeous—and he held the key to her happiness so long as he had the deed to her farm.

No, bad Ellie.

She wasn't going to sleep with him just because he owned the farm.

She wanted to slap her hands over her cheeks at that thought. Sleep with him? Where the heck had that come from? Ellie did not do casual sex. Not ever. She never had.

But she was tempted to start...

CHAPTER NINE

"**S**he okay?"

Ellie jerked her head up to find Max standing in the barn aisle. She and Lacey had fed the horses and Lacey was down at the other end, tugging the hose from stall to stall and filling water buckets.

"So far, so good," she said, smiling. She'd been sweeping up the tack room and checking bridles and saddles to make sure everything was in good order for her clients. The barn cats took care of the rats pretty good, but you never knew when one would take a shine to leather and get past them.

"What can you tell me about that guy?"

Ellie frowned. "He's not coming out here, Max. I promise."

"I believe you. But he's not going to stop harassing Lacey because of me."

Ellie sighed. "No, probably not. I don't think he'd physically hurt her—but he's mentally abusive. Always has been. They dated for six months. He was sweet as could be to her at first. Attentive, kind, always interested in what she was interested in. Hell, he came out here and watched her ride—

94

though sometimes I caught him checking his phone instead. Still, I figured it was typical guy stuff. Boyfriends aren't interested in horses necessarily. And when you don't understand how difficult training and showing can be, watching a horse perform can be boring. We ride in circles. I get that. You need to be an aficionado to understand it."

She sighed. "He was interested though. He said all the right things. And then he didn't. It was little stuff at first. Calling her at all hours to ask where she was and if she was with anyone. Then he'd apologize profusely and tell her he was afraid of losing her. She'd swear she wasn't going anywhere. But then he got careless and sent her a text meant for someone else—he talked about their hot date and the sex they'd had in a hotel, but it wasn't Lacey he'd been with."

"Ouch."

Ellie leaned against the doorjamb. "Yeah. He swore it was a onetime mistake and it would never happen again. Then he showed up with an engagement ring at her work. He thought that would do the trick, but Lacey told him to fuck off. He's been harassing her since."

"She should get a restraining order."

"She should, but she's convinced it won't fly. Brice runs a construction business, and he's made a lot of money. He's on the city council, and he contributes heavily to police causes."

Max was frowning. "I'll take care of it."

Ellie's heart skipped a beat. "What do you mean, you'll take care of it?"

He shrugged then, the fierce look on his face softening as if he hadn't meant her to see it. "I know people. She needs to file for the restraining order. I'll make sure it happens."

Ellie knew her jaw was hanging open. "How can you do that?"

The sudden grin he gave her was seriously sexy. And confident. "Trust me."

It hit her that she did. How could Max Brannigan *not* know people? He said he didn't have a fortune of his own, but he was *still* a Brannigan. And he was a badass Navy SEAL. Well, *former* SEAL.

"Okay."

One eyebrow arched. "Okay? Just like that?"

She couldn't help but grin. "Well, yeah. Just like that."

The look on his face grew suddenly intense, and her insides squeezed tight. His gaze had settled on her mouth, and her lips tingled. Her nipples tightened and her core grew hot and achy.

No, Ellie. Not now.

Yes, now.

It had been so long and she'd been so lonely.

"You need to stop looking at me like that, Ellie." His voice was a sexy growl that shivered through her nerve endings.

"Like what?" Now why did she have to sound so breathless? The horses munched their grain, and Lacey dragged the hose farther down the aisle, talking to the horses as she filled their buckets.

"Like I'm a hero."

Her breath hitched. "Aren't you?"

He stepped into the tack room, and the space seemed to grow suddenly smaller. He was big and tall and she felt his presence keenly.

"No. I'm a man, Ellie. I have faults, and I have desires."

Her heart was tapping out a staccato rhythm. "You do? Er, um—"

Now what, Ellie?

Did she ask him what those desires were? Did she assume he meant her? Did she close her eyes and purse her lips?

God no, that was silly!

He was there in front of her, his big body overwhelming but not threatening. He lifted a hand and she thought he might touch her face. She closed her eyes, leaned into it—

But he didn't. He backed away, and she opened her eyes to find him standing in the door where he'd originally been.

"You're a beautiful woman, Ellie Applegate. But you deserve more than what I want to give you."

Her breath shortened. *Dammit.* "What do you want to give me, Max?"

One corner of that gorgeous, sensual mouth quirked up. "Don't you know?"

Heat slid through into her bones, her blood. "Not really, no."

His laughter surprised her. "God, Ellie—you're too sweet. You aren't prepared for the likes of me, I promise you that."

Okay, so that statement pissed her off. "How do you know what I'm prepared for? You're unbelievable! Think you're God's gift to women or what?" She sniffed. "For your information, I'm not interested in deciphering whatever the hell you mean. And I'm not interested in *you*, either."

His gray eyes sparkled with humor. "You go ahead and tell yourself that, baby. If it makes you feel better."

Then he stepped out of the tack room and swaggered down the aisle. Ellie battled with herself not to cuss him out and call him back and run after him all at the same time.

He was just a man, damn him. A sexy, infuriating man that she did not want or need.

You go ahead and tell yourself that, baby. If it makes you feel better.

Ellie picked up the broom and attacked the dust as if it had personally insulted her.

No, she did *not* feel better. Not even close.

U

Max planned to stay away from the women, but Lacey came to his room when he was sanding the plaster and asked if he'd have dinner with them. She looked so hopeful and sweet that he couldn't say no. Even though he knew Ellie was probably pissed at him.

Jesus, what had he been thinking earlier when he'd stalked her in that tack room? She'd looked so sexy and receptive that he'd stepped into the room before he'd thought twice about it. He'd been planning to kiss her—but then she'd closed her eyes and tilted her face up to his and he'd been hit with her sweetness and vulnerability.

He had no right to take advantage of that, especially since he wasn't planning to stay any longer than it took to get her to sell.

"All right," he told Lacey. "Give me a few minutes."

He'd gone into town and gotten an air mattress, which he'd inflated earlier. He'd carried the old mattress outside and thrown it in the dumpster. There was no saving that musty, uncomfortable thing. He'd had to buy sheets and a blanket—and he'd even bought a new pillow. Yeah, so he was accustomed to sleeping in the dirt and sand and mud, but since he wasn't downrange, what was the point in being uncomfortable?

He put down the sander and ran the tacky cloth over the wall one more time. He told himself he was simply working to improve his prospects of a sale, but in reality it was something to do that took his mind off what he could be doing instead.

Max went and washed his hands, then followed the scent of fried chicken into the kitchen where he found Ellie at the stove and Lacey setting the table with three plates and three glasses. She smiled when he walked in and he returned the smile. Ellie did not turn around.

"I begged Ellie to fry up her momma's chicken," Lacey said. "Comfort food."

Ellie had two splotches of color on her cheeks when she turned and handed Lacey a basket of fried chicken. She didn't even look at him as she turned back to the stove and stirred something on the burner.

"We've got mashed potatoes and gravy, fried okra, and sliced tomatoes too," Lacey said. "I hope you're hungry."

"I am," he replied. For more than food, but he wasn't adding that part.

Goddamn, since when had he gotten to the point where he couldn't stop thinking about a woman? He'd never even kissed her, so why did she take up so much space in his head?

Because you want to kiss her.

Yeah, he wanted to.

He sat where Lacey told him.

"Want a beer?"

"Sure."

She popped the top off a Bud Light and set it in front of him. Then she helped Ellie get the bowl of potatoes and the pan of gravy on the table. A platter of tomatoes appeared along with the okra. Fragrant biscuits arrived with a stick of butter on a dish and a knife.

Lacey grinned as she sat down. "Ellie's feeling soft toward me, so I asked for my favorites."

Ellie pulled the red polka-dot frilly apron that was faded with age over her head and dropped it on the counter before she walked over and joined them at the kitchen table.

"You're a terrible friend," she said. "Taking advantage of me like this."

But Max could hear the love in her voice. It was one of the things he liked so much about her. She was prickly, but her feelings ran deep. The prickliness was like a porcupine's spines—meant to scare off predators before they went for her soft underbelly.

"I know," Lacey replied. "But you love me anyway."

"Not if you don't eat all this up." Ellie's voice was teasing.

"Max is going to help. Aren't you, Max?"

His mouth was watering and his stomach growled. "I think I can do some damage."

Lacey took a piece of chicken and then handed him the basket. He took two. Once they'd filled their plates, he dived in. The chicken was perfect.

"This is amazing, Ellie," he said after he had a bite of mashed potatoes and gravy.

For the first time since the barn, she met his gaze. "Thank you. I'm glad you like it."

Like it? He loved it. In some ways, this reminded him of family meals when his mother was still alive. He didn't think she'd actually cooked for their large family, but she'd certainly directed what happened in the kitchen. They'd always gathered at the table and shared what they'd been doing that day. For him and his brothers, it was much the same things—riding bikes, playing outside, playing video games, and all the other things boys did. For his father, it had been his work at the studio unless he'd taken time off to stay at home and do stuff with them. Which he'd often done before Mom had died.

And Mom? What had she done? Max couldn't remember. Finn had been so young then that most of her day had probably consisted of watching him more than the rest of them, but it bothered him he couldn't recall even a single thing she'd spent her days doing besides taking care of their every need. Oh, of course she'd played with them. He remembered that. But what else?

He didn't know.

He'd been nine by the time she died—it wasn't a crime to be unable to remember when everything was so dramatic and self-indulgent at that age, and yet it bothered him he couldn't.

"Ellie's momma used to win the first-place ribbon at the county fair with this recipe. No one could touch the Applegates when it came to chicken."

"Granny won for years before Momma took over."

"Do you enter now?" Max asked.

Ellie shook her head. "No time. I'm always too busy on the farm to take time off."

He was beginning to understand just how much she'd been doing by herself. She had Miguel, and Lacey helped her when she could. But it was a lot of work for one person to coordinate and keep up with.

Lacey changed the subject then, and they ate and talked about so many things over the next hour. Lacey wanted to know about growing up in California, and then they moved on to horse shows and what was next for Champ. Ellie asked if he'd like another beer and when he said he'd get it, she got up before he could do it himself.

"My legs aren't broke," he said when she set it down in front of him.

"No, but you're a guest here even if you do own the place, so shut up and accept the hospitality. By this time next week, I won't do it anymore, so enjoy it while you can."

He had the strongest urge to grab her arm and tug her into his lap so he could bury his hands in her hair and kiss her senseless. If they were alone, he thought she might even let him.

He watched her walk back to her seat. Lacey's eyes were on him when he reminded himself there were three of them in the room. She lifted an eyebrow and smiled knowingly. Yeah, she had his number when it came to Ellie. What could he do except shrug?

After they ate, he helped them clean everything up. Once that was done, Lacey suggested they sit on the porch and watch the sunset. Ellie looked on the verge of refusing as she glanced at him, but then she agreed and the three of them went outside and sat with their drinks. He knew he should probably go and leave them alone, but Lacey kept talking and asking his opinion from time to time, so he never managed to end his involvement in the conversation.

"Well, I'm beat," she said when the sun slipped behind the horizon, leaving only a pink glow. "Think I'll head up now."

"I thought we were going to watch a movie," Ellie said, clearly surprised by this turn of events.

"Next time. You stay here and keep Max company. I'll see you both in the morning."

It was silent after she left. And then Ellie laughed. "Well, *that* was subtle. Don't feel like you have to stay if you don't want to."

"I'm fine," he said. "But same goes for you. Don't stay if you want to go."

She picked up her drink. "No, it's okay."

"You didn't want to come out here at first, did you?"

She swung her head around to look at him. "Honestly? No, I didn't. I'm not quite sure what to think when it comes to you. It feels awkward sometimes—but it also feels like we've known each other for ages. I'm comfortable with you, and I'm not comfortable with you. If that makes sense."

He was surprised at how honest she could be with him. He liked it though. It's what made her so different from other women he'd been attracted to. He felt like with Ellie there were no games.

"I'm sorry for what happened earlier. In the barn. I shouldn't have said those things."

She shrugged. "What did you say that was so bad? You told me I shouldn't expect anything from you. There's nothing wrong with that. You thought I was interested, but I'm not. You don't have to worry."

She was so full of shit it was unreal. Her entire body vibrated with nervous energy just because he was near. She hadn't wanted him to join them for dinner, mostly because she hadn't wanted to sit in the same room with him across the table and think about what he'd said to her in the tack room.

The throaty growl in his voice. The flash of fire in his gray eyes. The flare of his nostrils as he'd told her not to look at him that way.

She'd asked him what way he meant, but she knew, didn't she? She'd been looking at him like he was something she wanted but couldn't have. Like he was out of her league because he came from so much more than she did, even if he was a Navy SEAL turned mercenary. He was still the son of a billionaire, and he still stood to inherit a fortune someday. Men like that did not settle for women like her.

She sniffed. As if she even *wanted* him to settle for her. And what did that mean, settle? She was strong and attractive, and she fried up a mean chicken dinner.

And you smell like you've been frying too. The kind of women he'd want would smell like perfume and old money, most likely. Not fried chicken and sweat (both human and horse), which is what she probably smelled like most of the time. Well, not the chicken part, but definitely the sweat. Add in horse shit and you had a combination guaranteed to win over the most handsome someday-billionaire you'd ever had the privilege of coming up against.

"I wasn't worried," he said, and her heart squeezed just a little bit.

She told herself she wasn't hurt. Wasn't disappointed. He'd said she was beautiful earlier. She hadn't imagined that. But maybe it was just his way of letting her down easy. She already knew he was a nice guy. He'd helped in the barn, and he'd stripped the carpeting from Granny's old room, and now he was fixing the walls. He didn't have to do any of that, even if he did own the place.

"That's good." What else could she say? "Lacey thinks the perfect solution to my dilemma is to make you fall in love with me. That's why she left us alone."

She had to give him *some* reason. She didn't want him thinking she'd asked Lacey to do it.

His gray eyes settled on her, and her heart kicked up. She took a sip of her drink and tried to act normal.

"What do you think, Ellie?"

She didn't pull her gaze from his. "I think it's a pretty good idea. *If* I had a clue how to go about it." She grinned, hoping he didn't take her too seriously. "But I don't, so you're safe."

"Thought you said you weren't interested?"

"In you, no. In this farm? Always."

He laughed. "At least you're honest. Mostly."

Her conscience pricked her. "What are you talking about, *mostly*?"

"You're definitely interested in the farm. I'd even say it's your number one priority. But Ellie, you aren't *un*interested in me."

She felt the heat flare beneath her skin. "You are so full of yourself. How do you make it through any doors?"

"My life sometimes comes down to accurately reading another person's intentions. I've gotten pretty good at it. You want me, but you don't want to want me. I can understand that because I've got the same feelings rattling around in my head about you. It's been a while since I've been with anyone, and you're lovely and warm and so tempting. But I'm not the right guy to erase your loneliness, Ellie."

She rocketed to her feet, her drink sloshing over the rim and splashing onto her hand. She didn't care. She wasn't going to accept this from him. Wasn't going to tolerate him sliding under her skin and digging out her deepest fears. She knew, on some level, it was an overreaction, that she should play it off and pretend he hadn't gouged a ragged line in her soul.

But she couldn't. She just wasn't made that way. She had to be strong so often, and carry so much, that she couldn't do it right now with him. Not anymore.

"You enjoy your night, Max. I'm going to bed where I don't have to listen to you sound so superior and smug. You own my farm, and there's nothing I can do about it. But you don't have the right to make assumptions about me just because you feel like you know it all."

He stood and caught her hand as she turned to go. She gasped in outrage—or was it the bolt of electricity sizzling through her that made it happen?

"Don't," he said. "Don't storm into the house pissed off at me for telling you the truth."

"You know nothing," she spat out. "Nothing at all."

Hot tears clogged her throat, but she wasn't going to let them fall.

"Oh yeah?" he snapped. With a growl, he yanked her into his arms. Her glass fell to the porch, rolling heavily across the boards. She had the impression of leashed strength and hard intensity as her palms went to his chest and curled into his shirt. But was she pushing him away or trying to pull him to her?

She would never know which because Max lowered his head and claimed her mouth with a beautiful savageness that thrilled her down to her toes.

CHAPTER TEN

What the hell was he doing? Max had vowed to himself—and to her—that he wasn't going to act on this attraction. He'd lied.

Ellie was soft in his arms. She'd been spitting mad when he'd grabbed her, but now she melted into him as he fitted his lips to hers and explored the sweetness of her mouth. Her lips parted and he slipped his tongue inside, stroking hotly against hers.

She made a noise in the back of her throat, but it wasn't one of protest. Her fists were curled into his shirt, and then her palms flattened and her arms slid up and around his neck. He told himself this was madness, that he should stop kissing her, but he knew it wasn't likely. He fitted her body to his, pulling her in close and sliding a hand down her hip, over the curve of her bottom, tugging her in until she could feel what she did to him.

What *was* she doing to him? He was a disciplined man. He had to be. He dealt with deprivation and want, and he did it often and without any regrets. For someone in his line of work, discipline was critical.

Yet he couldn't seem to find his ability to deny himself where she was concerned. She drove him past the limits of his restraint, no matter how he told himself he wasn't giving in to the need to possess her. He'd been so proud of himself earlier. He'd backed away when he'd needed to, given her space, and he'd congratulated himself for it.

He was not congratulating himself right now. Instead, he was kissing her. Taking all the sweetness she would give him and demanding more. He feathered a hand across her collarbone, circled her neck to cup her head.

He felt the rat-a-tat-tat of her pulse, hammering hard and fast in her throat, and his need to conquer and tame evolved into the need to protect and cherish. Whatever was happening between them, Ellie was still vulnerable beneath all the prickliness. He had to remember that.

He gentled the kiss and she followed his lead. Her tongue stroked against his softly, sweetly. He brought his other hand up to cup her head, his fingers sliding into her silky hair. She did not try to back away from him, and that pleased him as much as it pricked his conscience for kissing her in the first place.

He broke the kiss and pressed his forehead to hers. He could hear her breathing in the darkness, feel her soft breath on his lips.

He brushed his fingers against her neck again. Her pulse still raced, but so did his. He was uncomfortably hard too.

"Why did you stop?" she asked, and his gut clenched tight.

Yeah, why had he stopped?

"I stopped because I don't want anything between us to start with anger. We were pissed off at each other, and that's no way to begin."

Her hands were on his biceps, holding him lightly while he continued to cup her head in his hands.

"I shouldn't admit this, but I liked kissing you."

God, just when he thought she couldn't surprise him any more than she already had. "I liked kissing you too. I'm sorry I upset you."

"I think your destiny is to upset me, Max Brannigan. But that's okay because I'm tough. I'll get over it."

"So what do we do now, Ellie?"

Because it was up to her. He wasn't pushing her into anything. Hell, he shouldn't be asking her at all. He'd kissed her and he needed to let this go.

But he didn't want to. There was something about kissing her. Something so sweet and pure, and he wanted more of it. He hadn't had any sweetness in his life lately. He wanted that—*her*—with a fierceness that surprised him.

"I think I need to go to bed."

His entire body stiffened with need, but logically he knew she wasn't suggesting he go with her.

"And I need to consider what I really want," she finished.

"I understand."

Her hands moved up to his wrists, and she squeezed for just a second before stepping back and out of his grip. His fingers itched to touch her again, but he dropped his arms to his sides and didn't move.

"So I guess we understand each other now," she said. "Neither one of us is as immune as we'd like to pretend, are we?"

"Nope."

She nodded firmly. "So no more of this crap about who deserves what, right?"

The urge to sweep her into his arms and carry her upstairs was strong. What a woman. She went toe to toe with him and didn't back down. He loved that about her.

"That's right."

"I'll do my own thinking and you do yours. No deciding what's *best*"—she air-quoted the word—"for anyone but yourself. Got it?"

"Believe me, I got it, Ellie."

"Good."

He didn't know what to expect from her, but when she stepped up and stood on tiptoe to kiss his cheek—well, that wasn't it at all.

"Good night," she whispered.

The next few days were so busy that Ellie didn't see much of Max. Okay, strike that—she saw him, but they didn't spend any time alone together. Which was probably a good thing for her heart. She hadn't stopped thinking about that kiss since it happened. She'd been so furious with him, but the way she'd melted into him when his mouth touched hers had eradicated all her anger and replaced it with sizzling desire.

She'd wanted to keep kissing him. She'd wanted more than that, as well.

But she'd gone to bed instead. The next morning she'd gone with Lacey to the police department. Max had promised that he'd take care of making sure a restraining order stuck, so Ellie pushed until Lacey agreed to go. Ellie didn't know what he'd done, but the judge signed the order, and Brice was served later that day. He hadn't come within sighting distance of Lacey since then, though the official hearing was still a few days away.

Brice was an asshole, but when push came to shove, he was more worried about his own skin than he was about controlling Lacey. Ellie fretted about it, but Lacey insisted on going back home and back to work at the salon. She was sunny and bubbly again, and Ellie was happy for that even if she didn't trust that snake in the grass Brice.

She'd thought she'd see Max the day Lacey went home. She'd worried all day over how to behave that night when they were alone, but Max wasn't there. He'd left his cell number in case she needed him, but he went into town and didn't return until she was lying in bed reading. She thought about getting up and going to see if everything was okay, but then she decided that he was a grown man, she wasn't his mother, and it wasn't her business.

No matter that she'd lain awake for hours after he'd come in, wondering where he'd been. She'd been no good on Champ the next day. Miguel had frowned at her from the side of the ring.

"Ellie, what's the matter with you? You ride that horse like a sack of potatoes today! That show is next week, girl! Get it together!"

112

She had ridden pretty badly. Champ had sensed her distraction and tested her to the limit, as horses always did when you gave them any provocation. Give a horse an inch and he'd take a mile if you didn't stop him.

She'd fallen into bed that night far earlier than usual, and the next day she'd only seen Max long enough to wave from a distance. He'd worked in the house and then left later that afternoon for a few hours. But she was busy with lessons and training, so she mostly didn't notice him coming and going. All she knew was that the house was empty when she got up to it each night and he wasn't there.

It was the fourth night after their kiss when she went trudging up to the house from the barn. Her mind was on the broodmare she and Miguel had brought into the foaling area of the barn a couple of days ago. She was a young mare and this was her first foal, so Ellie worried more than she typically did about the veterans. She was planning to spend the night down at the barn in case the mare foaled that night, which Miguel thought likely, but first she wanted to grab something to eat and have a shower.

Miguel had offered to stay with her, but she'd told him to go home and promised to call if she needed him. He was only five miles away, so he could get there quickly. But he had a family, and she couldn't pay him for extra time anyway.

When she stepped into the house, she smelled food. Her stomach growled as she followed the scents back to the kitchen. Max was there, and he looked up when she entered, his gray eyes meeting hers for a long moment before he turned back to what he was doing.

"I stopped at Mary Lou's and picked up dinner," he said as he took food from containers and fixed two plates.

She could kiss him. Literally, right now, she could kiss him. But that would probably confuse the situation more than it already was, so she settled for a big smile. "You are a fantastic man," she said. "I might even love you right now."

He laughed as he carried over the plates and set them on the table. "Are you telling me that the way to your heart is through your stomach?"

She sat down and sniffed Mary Lou's meat loaf. Her mouth watered. "Right now, yes I am."

"What do you want to drink? Beer? Tea? Water?"

"A beer sounds good."

He retrieved two beers and joined her. He opened them up, handed one to her, and then clinked bottlenecks with her before taking a sip of his. She did the same. The beer went down cold and good. The meat loaf was going to go down even better.

She dived in and practically moaned at the first bite. She'd been planning on heating a frozen dinner in the microwave and heading back to the barn, so this was heaven. Sheer heaven.

"Hungry?" Max asked with a laugh.

"You have no idea." She forked up some mashed potatoes and gravy.

"How'd it go today? Busy?"

"Yes. Got a new student. A ten-year-old who's never ridden before—but she took to it pretty well. I'll have her posting in a week. Wait—do you even know what that is?"

He grinned. "I do, in fact. Mom explained it one summer when we'd gone on a family vacation. She'd been the only one to insist on an English saddle when we went trail riding. I think it was probably Luke who asked her why she was bouncing up and down—so she explained. I don't know why it stuck in my head, but it did."

Ellie was still focused on the part he'd said about trail riding. "So you've ridden before, huh?"

Max waved his fork. "Don't get any ideas. Those horses were nags. Yours are not."

She couldn't help but laugh. "Definitely not. But we could go over to the Kentucky Horse Park sometime—they have trail horses. You can tour the park on a horse."

"No thanks. Horses are your deal, not mine. If I don't need a key to fire up the horses under the hood, I'm not interested."

"Coward." She was only teasing him, but it was kind of fun.

"I don't know how you make them do what you want. It's not brute strength, that's for sure."

"No. More or less, you trick them into thinking you're the boss. If they ever get it in their heads that you aren't, you're in trouble."

"But you aren't worried about that, are you?"

She smiled. "I'm really not."

They continued to chat while they ate. It was nothing important, but it was nice. She was so accustomed to eating alone most of the time that having company was a welcome change. After they finished, she sat back, her stomach full and happy. Her body was so tired tonight, but she still had work to do. She pushed back from the table and Max looked at her questioningly.

"This was great, Max, really. But I have to get back down to the barn," she said, her blood humming from the little jolt of alcohol.

"You're going down to the barn? Do you need help with something?"

"I'm spending the night there. I've got a cot in an empty stall and—"

"Wait a minute—you're sleeping in the barn? Why?"

He looked confused and concerned. Warmth flowed through her at that look. *It doesn't mean anything, Ellie.*

No, it didn't. But it was still nice.

"Lily's going to foal soon. Might be tonight. I need to be there."

He sat back, surprise on his face. "You never stop, do you? There's always work to be done."

She smiled. "That's right." She shrugged. "Horses. It's what you do when you love them."

He shoved back from the table. "Let me help you, Ellie."

She had to blink for a second. He was talking about right now, not in general. Not forever.

"You already have. You brought me dinner. And it was terrific, by the way."

For some reason, she reached out and grabbed his hand. Squeezed. He squeezed back.

"Thanks, Max. I really appreciate it."

"You going straight back?"

"Taking a quick shower to wash off the dirt of the day. But then I'm going down."

His expression was fierce. "I'll take care of the dishes. Meet you on the porch in ten minutes?"

She shook her head as happiness washed through her. "You don't have to go. I appreciate it, but it's going to be cool in the barn tonight—and there are probably rats scurrying around in the darkness. You don't want to be there for that."

He laughed. "Rats? Is that all you've got? Honey, unless they've got AK-47s, I'm good. Meet you in ten."

The mare looked uncomfortable as hell. Max stood outside the stall with Ellie, who was frowning as she watched the horse pace and swish her tail. The stall she was in was far bigger than the other stalls. Ellie had explained it was a special stall just for having babies.

"She's sweating now, poor sweetheart. It could be anytime." Then she snorted. "Or not. You can never tell with one hundred percent accuracy."

"What do you have to do when it starts?" Max had never been present for a horse's birth before.

"Nothing much unless she gets into trouble. We're just here to make sure everything happens as it should. If the baby breeches, I'll have to help her. Otherwise, we're going to let Mother Nature do her thing. But I want to be close because this is her first. If she rejects the foal for some reason... Well, I'll need to get in there and make sure she doesn't hurt him or her. Then I'll have to get one of the nurse mares and hope we can bond the baby to her."

He'd had no idea it was so complicated. Beside him, Ellie yawned. He turned his head to look at her. Her face was in profile, small chin, upturned nose, long eyelashes, full lips. Lips he'd kissed a few nights ago. Lips he wanted to kiss again.

"Why don't you try to get some sleep? I can watch and wake you if something happens."

That's why he'd insisted on joining her. She'd looked so tired, and he'd known she was going to sleep down here with an alarm going off every so often so she could check on the horse. If he was here, he could watch and she could sleep longer.

Her gaze flicked over him and then back to the mare. "It could be a long time yet."

"That's why we can take turns. You sleep first."

"I don't know…"

"Ellie." He waited until she met his gaze. Green eyes rimmed with long, lush lashes stared back at him. It took everything he had to make himself concentrate on what he'd been planning to say. "I've spent countless nights on watch during missions. You can trust me. There, the penalty for fucking up was certain death. You can be sure that I take the mission seriously and that I'll guard that horse's life as if it were my own."

A small smile played on her lips then. He wanted to press his mouth to hers and taste it. "I think that's a little overboard, but I appreciate the sentiment." Her jaw cracked in another yawn. "Okay, I'll go first. Wake me in an hour or if her water breaks—or, if you don't see that happen, wake me if she lies down and doesn't get up again in a few minutes."

He put a hand over his heart. "Aye, aye, skipper."

Her frown was cute. "Skipper?"

"It's what sailors call the boss."

"Ah, got it. Sorry, kinda slow on the uptake right now."

He took the chance of pulling her into his arms. (A) because he wanted to. And (b) because she looked like she needed someone to hold her for a moment. She didn't push away, and he took that as a good sign. "Get in that stall with your cot and go to sleep. I'll sit right here."

There were folding chairs and a small table where he could set a drink and his phone.

She sighed, her fingers curling into his shirt. "You're a good man, Max Brannigan. You might even be a good horse-farm owner by the time we're through."

Through? He didn't like to think of them being through when they hadn't even begun. And then he wondered where the hell that notion had come from. She was a sweet, sassy, gorgeous woman he wanted to know intimately. But it was only sexual attraction. That's all it could be. He hadn't known her long enough to want anything else from her.

To put an end to his thoughts, he kissed her. Warm lips, wet tongue, hot breath. His cock grew hard, and he worked to remind himself that now wasn't the time. He broke the kiss and she sighed, her eyelashes fluttering open.

"That was nice," she said.

"I've got more where that came from. But I'm afraid the supply of nice is limited. Most of what I have left is hot and dirty and insanely pleasurable."

He watched her pupils dilate. Then she closed her eyes and muttered something to herself. He didn't have to ask what it was when her voice grew stronger.

"Five... Six... Seven..."

"What are you doing?"

Her eyes popped open again as she finished the count. "Counting to ten for patience. What does it look like?"

He shook his head. "No idea... What's the patience for, anyway?"

"It's so I don't ask you to show me all those things right here, right now."

CHAPTER ELEVEN

Ellie didn't want to wake up, but someone was gently shaking her and calling her name. A masculine voice. That was unusual, wasn't it? She didn't have a man in her life…

She jerked awake, her heart pounding. "Max?"

"I'm right here. I think something's happening."

Ellie pushed herself upright, her mind fuzzy, her body protesting the rude jump into wakefulness. Max's hand was there above her, and she grabbed on, let him pull her to her feet. She only swayed a second before she headed for Lily's stall.

"When did this start?"

"One thirty-three and ten seconds."

She stumbled to a stop. "One thirty-three and—you didn't wake me after an hour!"

"No, I didn't. You needed the sleep, and I don't, so there was no point. And I did exactly what you said and came to get you when something changed. She lay down and didn't get up again. She's breathing heavily too."

Ellie rushed to the stall and looked in. Lily was on her side, legs extended, sides heaving. Ellie went to the bucket of antiseptic solution she'd prepared and washed her arm in it. Then she grabbed the towel she'd set there and dried off before putting on a sterile glove.

"What do you need me to do?" Max asked.

"Just stay here. I'm going to check that the baby is in the right position, then we'll need to leave her alone and watch."

Lily snorted softly as Ellie went inside the stall, but she didn't try to stand. Ellie went over and patted her side, then worked her hand down to the mare's perineal area. Her water had broken and her legs were wet with it. Ellie worked her hand inside the mare, feeling gently forward into the birth canal. She felt a hoof, and her pulse skipped a little higher.

"Easy, sweetheart," she said as she felt for the other hoof. And there it was, along with a nose. Thank God.

She eased her arm back before another contraction ripped through the mare.

"That's a girl," she said as she stood. "You're almost there."

She left the stall and closed the door behind her.

Max was standing there with a concerned look on his face. "Is she okay?"

For some silly reason, her heart squeezed so tight that it hurt. He genuinely seemed like he cared about what happened to the mare lying on her side in so much pain. And that meant that she couldn't help but adore him in that moment.

"Yes. It's her first time, so I'm more cautious than I would be with one of the other mares, but the baby is in the right position. And Lily's in a good position too. Not too close to a wall or door. I'll have to watch her from now until the baby is born, but if you want to go, you can."

He looked at her like she was crazy. "Why would I want to go? Is she having a baby or what?"

"She definitely is. Not long now." Ellie felt the joy of the moment bubbling up inside her. Why was she so happy? She'd been through this many times before, but this moment was different. Because Max was here.

A sudden wave of sadness washed over her at the thought of her mother. How many mares had she witnessed foal with Momma at her side? How many dreams and plans had they hatched in the middle of the night while waiting for a new life to arrive? Something of what she felt must have shown on her face because Max reached out and skimmed his fingers over her cheek.

"You okay?"

She smiled brightly. "Yes. Fine." Her eyes teared up though and she turned away, pulling at the glove. "I need to get rid of this."

She disposed of the glove and returned to the stall. Max was watching Lily's sides heave, his attention rapt on her.

"Thanks for letting me sleep," she said. She felt him look at her, but she kept her attention on Lily.

"I thought you'd be mad."

"I'm not. You did the most important thing, which was tell me when something changed. I'm only sorry you had to spend the past few hours alone with so little to do."

He chuckled softly. "I keep telling you, babe, this is nothing. I know how to spend hours doing next to nothing while keeping watch. This is actually far more pleasant than any of those nights were."

She couldn't help but turn to face him. "Why would a man like you do such a thing? Seems as if you'd have the world at your feet if you wanted it."

He looked down at her. "I didn't want it. My father was a workaholic. After my mother died, we hardly saw him. He traveled and he worked late, and he never knew how to let go and have fun the way he once did. Mom was the love of his life. He lost his parents when he was a teenager, and he lived in darkness until she came along. When he lost her, he went back to that darkness."

He shrugged. "I guess all of us boys have some of the same darkness within us. I didn't know what I wanted when I left home at eighteen. I went to college for a while. All we did was drink and party—but one night, when I was sick of drinking beer and feeling like shit, I got caught up in a movie. Charlie Sheen was in it and it was about Navy SEALs. I remember thinking, 'That right there is what I want to do.' So I left school and went to the recruiter's office."

"Just like that, huh?"

He snorted. "Definitely *not* just like that. You have no idea how hard it is to become a SEAL. And you don't get to apply right away either. So I did my time in the regular Navy and then I applied. One of the instructors figured out that I was one of *those* Brannigans. They teased the shit out of me, thought I'd quit, but all that did was harden my resolve."

"And you made it."

"I made it. Proudest day of my life."

She loved listening to him talk. He had a voice that sounded like fine whiskey and the kind of rocks you find at the bottom of a river—smooth, deep, and strong. Maybe that was a silly way to imagine it, but it made sense to her.

"So why did you leave the Navy?"

She didn't imagine the tightening of his jaw in the dim light of the barn. Or the way his fingers curled around the bars of the stall. "It was time to go."

"Yet you went to work doing the same thing for someone else. Or did I misunderstand you?"

"You didn't."

He didn't say anything else, and she didn't push him. Clearly, she'd asked him enough questions and he wasn't going to answer that one.

Just then a tiny hoof popped out. "Look," Ellie said, grabbing Max's arm. "The baby's coming!"

It didn't take long at that point. A few heaves and the baby slid most of the way out. The back legs were still inside, but the membranes had broken and the foal was breathing on its own. One less thing for her to worry about.

Another contraction hit and the baby was free, a slick little thing lying on the straw. Ellie slid the bolt to the stall and went inside. She picked up straw and dried the newborn colt while Lily pushed herself up and started to lick him.

"What happens now?" Max asked from the other side of the door.

"It'll take a little while for him to stand and nurse. I have to keep watch for that—and then there's the placenta. Once she passes it, I have to make sure it's intact. The vet will come by tomorrow to examine everyone."

Ellie sat back on her heels and sighed as Lily nosed her baby. Ellie hadn't been sure what the mare would do the first time, but Lily seemed to accept everything that had happened. Instinct was taking over and helping prod her in the right direction, and that was good.

Ellie left the stall and joined Max. "Thanks for coming out here with me tonight," she said, her eyes on the mama and baby instead of him. "I appreciate it."

He reached out and gently put a hand on her face, turning her to look at him. Her skin tingled where he touched, and her breath shortened as if he somehow had control of that too.

"You're a remarkable woman, Ellie Applegate. I'm glad I was here with you."

"Don't make me cry, Max. I'm already halfway there. I always get emotional when my mares have their babies."

"Duly noted. Hey, you want me to run up to the house and grab some coffee?"

"That's the best idea I've heard all night."

He grinned. "Be right back then."

Ellie settled into a chair to wait. She listened to his footsteps fade away, and then she tilted her head back and listened to the soft sounds of the barn at night. Caesar appeared from nowhere and rubbed against her legs, meowing as he did so. She reached down to scratch him and he started to purr. Misty, another of the barn cats, ambled out of the darkness with a mouse in her teeth. After a look at Ellie, she trotted into the shadows to dispose of her prey.

Ellie sighed. This was her life. Horses, barn cats, the smell of sweet hay and grain and leather. She didn't want it to change. And yet she knew change was coming. It was inevitable, in fact. One way or the other, the man who'd left to fetch some coffee was going to change everything.

But would the change be good or bad? That's what she didn't know.

U

Max thought that Ellie would go to sleep and stay in bed for a few hours after the disjointed sleep of last night, but he was wrong. They'd left the barn around four and gone back up to the house. They didn't say much as they went their own way, but there wasn't much to say at that time of the morning anyway.

At five thirty, he heard her rattling around upstairs. By a quarter till, the back door banged shut and he knew she was off to the barn to feed. He got dressed and went to help her. Miguel was there, and he grinned as Max approached.

"*Amigo*, you are back for more?"

Max laughed. "I'm beginning to realize the work is never done."

"No, that is true."

Ellie smiled at him. He liked it when she smiled. Max went to grab hay and gave each horse their ration as Ellie scooped grain. The mama and baby were looking happy and healthy in their stall. The baby nursed and the mama munched her feed. Then the baby bounced around a bit, twisting his long, spindly legs and hopping. Such a fragile thing, and so full of energy at the same time.

Ellie put the wheelbarrow away and then returned with a tiny halter. She and Miguel went into the stall and put the halter on the baby, who didn't seem too happy about the situation but went along with it anyway.

"You have to handle them right away," Miguel said to Max. "Get them used to people and let them know they have work to do."

"It starts early then."

"Better now than when he's bigger and stronger."

"Miguel's specialty is handling the babies," Ellie said. "He'll have this little guy walking on a lead line and picking up his feet before too long."

She yawned, and Max frowned at the dark circles under her eyes. But he knew she wouldn't go back to bed. There were horses to take care of and clients to give lessons to, and she wouldn't hear of taking a rest and postponing those things.

Not that he supposed she had much of a choice. He still hadn't asked to see the books, but he figured that most of her money came from lessons and boarding. If she didn't give the lessons, she'd have less money in her budget.

Max stuck around to do what he could, but by midmorning it was clear he'd get more done at the house. Lacey arrived, her smile as sunny as ever, while Ellie was giving a lesson to a middle-aged woman who kept hunching over no matter how many times Ellie told her to sit up straight.

"Poor Terri," Lacey said. "She used to ride over fences, and she hasn't quite gotten the hang of saddlebreds yet. But she will!"

"Things okay at work and home?" he asked. He'd spent some time over the past couple of days watching her place for any signs of Brice, but the man hadn't appeared at all.

"They sure are," she said. "Thanks again for your help. He hasn't called me once."

"Be sure and tell me if he does, okay?" Because if he did, Max was making certain there were consequences.

"I will."

Max left her and went back up to the house. He was still working on the walls—Ellie had picked a color from the samples he'd gotten—and he wanted to finish. He'd buffed the floors, but he was thinking about stripping and sanding them before applying a new stain.

He told himself it was so the farm would sell when it was time, but deep down he knew that wasn't the real reason. Deep down, he wanted to please Ellie. He wanted to see her smile, and he wanted to ease some of her worry.

Except he was one of the big causes of her worry, wasn't he? Son of a bitch, nothing about this whole mess was easy. Had his dad known what he would find here? Or had he only hoped that Max would show up, meet Ellie, and want to help her out?

His dad hadn't talked a lot to him about being a SEAL. But he'd been proud. He'd said those words once when Max had been on leave. He'd been visiting California when his father called and asked him to go for a drink. They'd met at a bar that night, and his dad had ordered his favorite drink. Bushmills 21. Max preferred a good beer, but what the hell, he'd ordered one too.

The whiskey was smooth and strong, and he remembered thinking about how much it cost and how the guys he worked with wouldn't waste that much money on a single drink.

The meeting hadn't lasted long. Only long enough for the whiskey to disappear. Once that was gone, his dad had looked at his watch, said he had a meeting, shook Max's hand, and left. Typical Dad, always running to the next deal, the next big score.

But he'd said one thing that had stuck with Max.

"I'm proud of you, son. Of the man you've become. It takes more guts than I've ever possessed to do what you're doing. Keep protecting the world and making it a safer place—but protect yourself as well. When you decide you're done, I'll always have a place for you."

But Max had never been done. Not really. He didn't think he'd ever be done—except, in the dark of the night since he'd come to Kentucky, there was something about the quiet of the farm and the peacefulness of horses in the field. And something about the woman who worked her ass off to keep it all together.

He rubbed the back of his arm across his forehead to keep the sweat from dripping into his eyes and surveyed the walls. They were about as even as possible for old plaster walls, and they shone with new cream paint.

He dropped the roller onto the tray and stepped back. His first thought was to go get Ellie and show her. His second thought was that he needed to take a mental step back from the churning thoughts in his brain and try to gain some clarity.

He thought about calling Knox again—but Knox was happily in love and not about to understand Max's misgivings about Ellie and the farm. Instead, he decided to call James.

James was the oldest, and unlike the majority of their brothers, James wasn't going to let a woman change his life. Max, James, and Finn. They were the only sensible brothers left.

Max could use some sensible advice right now.

CHAPTER TWELVE

Ellie managed to get a quick nap in the afternoon, then it was back to the barn for more work. She didn't see Max when she went up to the house, though she smelled paint. His truck was gone, and she figured he'd had to go get more supplies. He'd been painting the room, and he'd managed to unstick the windows. She hoped, selfishly, he'd unstick them all before too long.

By the time she finished at the barn for the day, his truck was once more parked in the driveway beside hers. Her heart tapped a little faster as she walked up to the house. He was sitting on the back porch, which she discovered as she started up the steps and he spoke, making her jump.

"Sorry," he said. "Didn't mean to scare you."

"It's okay. I was kind of lost in my thoughts."

"How's the baby?"

She took the seat beside him and sank onto the cushions. The sun shone on the bluegrass, and she sighed with happiness.

"He's perfectly fine. The vet says he's strong and healthy. No anemia."

"That's good."

"It is." She tilted her head as she looked at him. "What have you been up to today?"

"Painting."

"I thought I smelled paint."

"Want to see?" He got up and held out a hand.

She put her hand in his and let him help her up. "Definitely."

She wished he'd keep holding her hand as they walked through the door and into the house, but he didn't. He led the way, and when he stepped into the room and turned back to her, she had an image of him always leading her to this bedroom and then turning to catch her as she walked into his arms.

Stop that.

She crossed her arms as she stepped inside and turned around to look at the walls. "Wow. What a difference this makes."

"You should see it during the day when it's brighter."

"I'm amazed."

"You picked the color."

"Yes, but you sanded and patched the plaster." Tears pricked her eyes. "I never thought this room could be elegant, but I think it could."

"Build a bathroom and it could be a hell of a master suite."

"I think you're right. Maybe someday."

She knew he heard what she didn't say. Someday, if she owned the farm and had the money.

He came over and stood before her, and her pulse skipped. She wanted to reach up and skim her fingers along his jaw, but she wouldn't do it. He confused her and aroused her, and she didn't quite know how to behave around him anymore. God, had he really only been here a few days? It felt like he'd been in her life forever.

"Ellie, I need to see the books. I need to know what you're taking in and what the expenses are."

She swallowed as her throat knotted tight. Well, *that* wasn't what she'd expected. But of course it was his right to see the finances for the farm he owned. He wasn't going to be lenient or generous, and she needed to remember that. This was about business, no matter that there was clearly an attraction between them too.

"Well then, I guess you should come to the office." Her voice sounded stilted, and she knew she wasn't hiding her emotions very well.

Max frowned. "I'm not trying to hurt you. I want to help. I want to do what's best for us both."

"Of course. I understand." She turned to go before she did something ridiculous like cry—and it *was* ridiculous, but she was tired and worn out and her emotions boiled right beneath the surface. She couldn't blame him for what he wanted, just as she couldn't blame herself for her own dreams. They were both caught in the middle, and there was no easy way out for either of them.

He caught her and spun her around again and she gasped. He held her by the shoulders, gently but firmly. There was something in his gaze, something hard and fierce and protective, and she had the strongest urge to melt into him and let him take care of everything.

But that's not what she did. She was a fighter, and she didn't give up. Not ever.

"You don't believe me, do you? After everything, you think I'm going to rip the rug out from under you."

"Aren't you?"

His gaze dropped to her mouth, and her insides sizzled with awareness. "I called my oldest brother. He's a businessman, the kind of guy who sizes everything up based on dollar signs and how much money he stands to gain. He told me to take an inventory and put the place on the market—with or without your permission—because once you see the amount of the check you stand to gain, you won't refuse to sign the papers when we have a buyer on the hook."

She snorted, but he put a finger over her lips before she could speak.

"I told him he didn't know you if he thought that was going to work. That I've never seen a more determined or stubborn woman in my life."

He pulled his finger away from her mouth, and she blinked in confusion. "You aren't planning to follow his advice?"

"No, I'm not. I want to see the books because I own the place and I have the right to know what's going on here. Yes, I want to sell it—but I want your agreement that it's the best thing to do."

She felt the tension in her body leaching away. For the moment, anyway. "Then come to the office and I'll show you."

"It can wait until you're rested. You look like you're about to fall asleep where you stand."

"I'm fine." She sighed. "Just let me go up and take a quick shower, and then I'll show you."

He let her go. "If that's what you want."

134

Without him holding her up, she did feel as if she might crumple to the floor and sleep for the next few hours.

"Just give me a few minutes." She started for the door, then turned back as if she'd forgotten something. "Thanks for all the hard work in here. It looks amazing. Almost as if you should be fixing up houses instead of fighting wars."

He frowned, a quick movement of his brows that transformed his whole face. It was over as fast as it happened and his expression was smooth. "You're welcome, Ellie."

U

What the hell had he been thinking? Max ran a hand over his head and blew out a breath. He should have worked up to the books in a different way, but it had been on his mind a lot lately. And even more so since he'd talked to James.

He could still hear James's voice in his head, telling him to put the place on the market anyway. That's what James was going to do with the winery he'd inherited. In fact, he'd recently let it be known through his contacts that he was taking offers on the place.

Max was surprised he hadn't sold the winery before now, but of course James was so busy managing all his many investments that a tiny Italian winery hadn't commanded much of his attention. Still, he would sell it without regret and move on to the next thing on his list.

Max knew that James's advice was sound—but he couldn't do that to Ellie. If he put the farm on the market and got an offer without her knowledge, she'd certainly never speak to him again.

He wished he was capable of not caring about that, but dammit, he did care. His mistake had been in staying once he came to check the place out. He snorted. It was almost as if Dad had known what would happen when he'd inserted that clause in the contract where Max had to visit the farm. If Max hadn't stayed, if he'd taken a look around, demanded to see the books, found out what he was dealing with, he could have then done precisely what James told him to do.

Yeah, but she wouldn't have gone along with it even if you presented her a buyer with a million in cash free and clear for her.

No, she wouldn't have. Ellie didn't think that way. She probably should, but she didn't. The farm meant something to her, and it was something more than what he'd thought at first, which was simply nostalgia and tradition.

She cared about the horses. Cared about Miguel and Lacey. Hell, she probably even cared about the students who came to take lessons and the people she bought grain and tack from. Ellie cared about people, not profit.

He heard the water running upstairs and he thought of her in the shower, water sluicing over her naked body. That didn't do much for his state of mind, but it did make him hard.

Shit, maybe he should have taken the time to let off a little steam before coming to Kentucky. He hadn't done so. He had a few women he could have called, women who didn't expect anything from him other than a few orgasms every once in a while when he was in town. But he'd opened the envelope, done an Internet search that told him nothing, and then climbed into his truck and headed west.

He'd wanted to deal with the farm and Ellie Applegate right away.

The water shut off and he pictured her reaching for a towel, drying her lush body, her brown hair wet and dripping. What the hell was he going to do about this farm? About Ellie? About the way he wanted to lay her down on a bed and explore every inch of her body?

It was damned inconvenient to have a hard-on for the woman he was supposed to be convincing to let go of her farm for both their benefits. His phone buzzed in his pocket and he took it out to see who was calling.

Ian Black. He'd told the former CIA agent that he wasn't taking any jobs for a while, but he answered anyway.

"Hey, man, what's up?"

"Wondering how it's going," Ian replied.

Max snorted as he walked toward the kitchen. He needed a beer. And maybe a spot on the porch where he could listen to the night sounds of the farm.

"It's going."

"You ready to come back to work?"

Ordinarily, Max would be champing at the bit—ha-ha—to head out for an adventure. A week in Kentucky shoveling shit, birthing horses, and renovating a house ought to have him on edge by now.

But he wasn't on edge. Or not because of shit and renovations.

"What do you have?" he asked, because he was programmed to want to know.

"Incursion in Acamar. We need boots on the ground to hold back the Freedom Force." Acamar had been volatile for quite some time—since neighboring Qu'rim had been undergoing a civil war. The Freedom Force was a group of terrorists that was widely believed to be fueling the rebellion. If they got a toehold in Acamar—well, that nation could fall too. "You're one of my best operators, Max. I know you've got shit to deal with, but we could use you."

"Give me some time," he said, though his gut ached at the thought and guilt at the idea of leaving tore through him. "I have to wrap some things up here first, but a stint in the desert sounds good. I'll get back with you as soon as I can, though it could be a couple of weeks or so."

"The sooner the better, man."

"Copy that. Over and out."

He didn't have to end the call because Ian had already done it. He sat there looking at the moon rising over the farm and outlining the horses in the pasture. It was so peaceful here. So beautiful. Did going to the desert really sound good? Or was he contemplating running from something he couldn't quite figure out?

"Are you leaving?"

He turned at the sound of her voice, cursing himself for not hearing her approach. Usually he heard everything. His life depended on it more often than not. But he'd been so wrapped up in the call and his thoughts that he'd missed it.

Which meant he was slipping, because now that she was here, he could smell her shampoo. She was wearing a robe that lay open, the ties dangling at her sides. Beneath that was a dark top that appeared to end somewhere above the waistband of the dark, formfitting pants clinging low on her hips. As if he needed to be reminded of her curves. Her arms were crossed beneath her breasts, wrapped around her body as she held herself. It was a defensive posture, and he wondered how much she'd heard. What she thought.

"I have to at some point," he said, because he had to be honest with her.

"That sounded like you were going sooner rather than later."

"Would you like that?"

He heard her suck in a breath. "I—" She hesitated. "Yes."

"That's what I thought."

"And no," she blurted. She came closer, standing over him where he sat in the chair. She smelled sweet and clean, and he wanted to tug her close and bury his face in her belly, which was at eye level. "If you're here, I worry about the farm and what's going to happen. If you go, then I think I have time and I can fix everything. But if you go... I'll miss you. It's crazy, but I kind of like having you around."

"When I don't piss you off, of course." He wanted to laugh even as a wave of relief washed through him. And then there was the strong urge to possess her that was beating a furious tempo in his brain.

"Of course."

"Ellie, I need to tell you something." Because it was getting more and more difficult to keep his hands off her. Especially now when he was so torn between the life he knew—a life of war and brutality—and the pastoral life that he was currently leading.

Her voice, when she spoke, sounded breathless, as if she had some indication of what he was about to say. Or maybe she simply felt the currents snapping between them too. "Yes?"

"If you don't want to end up naked in a bed with me to-night, you need to walk back inside that house right now."

CHAPTER THIRTEEN

Ellie's body melted, liquefying at his words—at the heat and need in them. Her breath lodged in her throat, and she felt like a rabbit caught in the headlights. Stay? Or run?

Running was sensible. Running would protect her. Her heart, her soul.

But staying—oh, staying was so damned tempting. Because what waited for her if she stayed? She already knew she was powerfully attracted to this man. She was primed and ready to go off at the slightest touch.

But was that safe? Was it sensible?

Of course it wasn't sensible. And possibly not safe considering the lonely state of her heart. He'd been talking about leaving. About going to the desert, and she was certain that wasn't a good place where fun things happened.

He'd been talking about going back to work. Putting himself in harm's way. She hated the idea.

"Ellie," he growled. A warning.

She didn't move. Didn't back away. Her nipples had tightened almost painfully, and she could feel the building heat between her legs. She ached and wanted and needed. So, so much. And if he left, she would never get it. Never find out.

"I'm not going." Her throat was tight as she said the words, but right now that was her truth. She wasn't going. And she didn't want him to go either. Not right now. And not anytime soon. Which was crazy, right?

But it was true.

He still didn't move. "You should. I can't promise you anything, Ellie. My life is chaotic. Dangerous and messy. I'm not the kind of man to stay anywhere for long."

She snorted. "I don't think I asked you to stay, did I?"

But a part of her soul ached at the thought he wouldn't. That he would pack up and leave her house and her life just as easily as he had come into it. And he wouldn't leave it for the better if he got his way and sold her farm, would he?

His voice was soft and smooth and determined. "Are you telling me that a hot and dirty fling is all you want? Because that's all I have to give."

She snorted. "For a man who warned me I needed to get into the house before he stripped me naked, you sure are spending a lot of time trying to talk me out of it. Maybe you're the one who doesn't know what you want, Max. You ever think of that?"

He rose in a fluid, graceful movement that managed to surprise her with its speed. And then he was towering over her, his body taking up so much of her personal space.

She shivered. Because that's all she could do. Would he touch her? Or would he continue to insist she didn't know what she wanted and walk away? The truth was that she didn't know. She couldn't predict what Max Brannigan would do at any given minute.

She decided she was tired of waiting. Hell, why should she wait when she'd decided she wanted this?

She stepped into him, wrapped her arms around his neck, and tugged his head down. He could have resisted her, she knew that, but he didn't. He let her lead him into the kiss.

And then he took over, as if the bands of his steely control had finally given way. He had his hands on her hips, tugging her into him, letting her feel every inch of his arousal. Ellie tried to press herself closer as the fireworks in her body started to burn and pop. These were only the preliminaries—she couldn't imagine how good the main event would be.

Suddenly, he reached down and cupped her behind, urging her up. She lifted her legs, put them around his waist—and her belly did a free fall into her toes. He was so big and strong, and she was next to nothing in his arms. She liked it.

He started moving, still kissing her, and then he broke the kiss and kicked the door open. He kicked it closed behind them and she laughed.

"Where am I taking you?" he asked, and she knew he wanted to know where she would be most comfortable. His room and the air mattress. Her room. A guest room.

God, she hadn't thought that far ahead—but somehow she knew she wanted to be in her room. Maybe that was a mistake—maybe, once he'd gone, she'd regret that she'd ever let him into her bed. And then she'd be forced to change rooms, and that would piss her off.

"Upstairs. Down the hall. Sixth door on the right."

He kissed her again, and she melted into him. It took a good ten minutes to get there because he kept stopping and kissing her, but they made it up the stairs and into her room. He strode over to the bed, dropping her backward and coming down on top of her. Her legs were still around him, and she realized with a groan just how perfect it was.

His cock rode the crease in her thighs, pressing into the sensitive spot that ached for his touch. She'd put on a pair of leggings and a crop top, then put her robe on over that before she'd gone to find him. Now she was wishing she'd put on the robe and nothing else.

Except how forward would that have been?

He kissed her thoroughly, slowly and deliciously, as if he had all the time in the world. She felt like *she* didn't have all the time though. She wanted more, and she wanted it now. But he wasn't going to be hurried.

He slipped the robe open and palmed her breast, his mouth still on hers. Still demanding and perfect. Excitement built inside her, made her squirm. Her body was on fire. She wanted his mouth in other places, not just on hers, but she also didn't want him to stop kissing her. It was a hell of a dilemma.

He ran a hand down her side, under the edge of her top, and then up beneath it, his fingers gliding against bare skin until he reached her bra. He pulled the cup down and toyed with her nipple, and she nearly came unglued.

He lifted his head and gazed down at her, a knowing and smug look on his face. "You like that?"

"Absolutely not," she said. "It's terrible."

He chuckled. "And you're a terrible liar, Ellie."

She couldn't help but grin. Now what the heck was she doing, lying beneath this man while he touched her so intimately and making jokes? He was going to think her cracked in the head if she didn't stop.

"I wonder what you would do," he murmured, "if I put my mouth there instead?"

"Why don't you find out?" The moment she said it, heat blazed through her—but was it embarrassment or anticipation? God knew she wasn't a virgin—but she wasn't exactly Miss Experience either.

He sat up, his knees on either side of her body, and put his fists on his hips. "This will work better if you get rid of that robe, you know."

She shrugged out of it as quickly as she could, her heart racing merrily along. He put his hands on the edge of her top and started to push it upward, revealing her skin slowly. She wanted to scream.

"Max."

He had a faraway look in his eyes when his gaze met hers. "What?"

"You can go a little faster."

He grinned. "Impatient?"

"If you must know, yes. It's been a long time for me—and I'm dying here."

His expression grew fierce. "How long?"

She swallowed. Well, she'd brought it up, hadn't she? "More than two years."

"More than— Jesus, Ellie. I had no idea."

"Well, why would you? And also, this talking thing is going on a little too long."

He reached for her top again and shoved it up and over her head as she lifted herself, whipping it off and dropping it on the floor. "I can fix that, honey. Believe me." He sat back a second. "But first, let me look at those gorgeous breasts."

145

She'd put on a black lace demibra before she'd gone downstairs, and she was very glad about that at the moment. The creamy swells of her breasts threatened to spill over the cups. One cup was askew since he'd tugged it down a moment ago. He reached out and tugged both cups down, exposing her nipples and causing her breasts to sit up high.

"Now that's a beautiful sight," he murmured. And then he pressed his palms to either side of her shoulders and levered himself down until his mouth was within inches of her nipples. "You sure about this, Ellie?"

Was she sure? Her body was strung so tight she thought she might scream if he didn't touch her—and even if he did. There were things skipping and jumping and clamoring for joy inside her that she had forgotten existed. Was she sure? Oh hell yes.

"Yes, Max. I'm sure. Please, *please* stop talking."

He laughed—and then he fastened his lips around one nipple, sucking it deep while she gasped and grabbed his shoulders with both hands. Oh, the sizzling torment streaking through her right now. Her body was like a bow, strung tight and ready to snap at his command.

He cupped her other breast with his hand, his thumb gliding over her neglected nipple while he continued to drive her insane with his mouth. He licked and sucked and teased—and then he moved to the other nipple while cool air chilled the one he'd just left.

She was wet. So wet and achy. So ready to feel him between her thighs, his hard body driving into hers and reminding her how wonderful sex could be.

She didn't know how long she was going to have to wait for that moment, but she wasn't unhappy with what he was doing now. Her nipples were far more sensitive to the touch of his mouth than she'd expected them to be.

He reached for the waistband of her leggings and dragged them downward. When he lifted himself off her to remove them, she helped. Now she was clad only in black lace panties and her bra, which currently did nothing to hide her breasts from his gaze.

"Wow," he said, and she blushed at his approval.

"I'd like to be wowed too," she replied. "If you'd care to remove a few things for me."

He reached down and grabbed the edge of his T-shirt with one hand, lifting it off in a smooth maneuver that managed to be sexy as hell. Her breath caught at the sight of his chest. She'd seen him shirtless the day he'd helped Miguel muck stalls, but that had been from a distance. Now?

"I'm wowed," she breathed, and he chuckled. She lifted a hand and touched hot skin. He was muscled, but not hugely so. Beautifully so, she'd say. There was a dark, shiny mark on his shoulder. Round. She bit her lip, frowning.

"An old gunshot wound," he said, and her belly squeezed tight. If he went to the desert, as the person on the other end of the phone earlier seemed to want, what might happen to him then?

He lowered his head and captured her mouth. She opened to him, their tongues tangling hotly. And then he stopped and gave her a look. "It's an *old* wound, Ellie. Emphasis on old."

Had she been that transparent?

"Yes, but that doesn't mean you're bulletproof. Or does it? Do they have suits for that now?" She kept her voice light and teasing, but yes, it worried her. She didn't know why that should be—except she liked him, dammit. Liked him a lot. Even though she shouldn't.

"I thought you didn't want to talk. Yet here you are, talking. A lot."

"Then make me stop, Max. Make it impossible to talk."

"Challenge accepted, babe. Hold on, because I'm about to rock your world."

He launched into a full frontal assault that took her breath away. He slid down her body, gliding his mouth down to the waistband of her panties. And then he slipped the black lace off her hips and over her knees. They disappeared somewhere, but she couldn't quite say where because he pushed her knees open and touched his tongue to her center and her mind went utterly blank.

"Damn, you're wet," he murmured before spreading her open with his thumbs and swiping his tongue over the delicate pink bud of her clit.

Ellie arched her back, her hips lifting off the bed. Her mouth opened but nothing intelligible came out. Max slid his tongue over her clit again and again, until she was nearly mindless with the pleasure building inside her. Her skin was hot, her body burned, and the temperature in the room went up a million degrees.

She felt a crisis gathering deep inside her, the tightening of her body that signaled release, the impossible heat and pleasure that bordered on pain because it hurt so good. She was desperate to come, and yet she wanted to prolong the moment as long as she could because it had been so long and she didn't want it to be over too quickly.

But Max was too good for that. He held her down, held her legs open, and licked her into oblivion.

She came in a rush, gasping for breath and moaning his name at the same time. Her body splintered and reformed and splintered again. He eased off her and sat on the side of the bed.

When she could form a thought, she turned to look at him. He stood and picked up his shirt, and little alarm bells started ringing in her head.

"Where are you going?" she asked, her voice hoarse and almost unrecognizable to her. Wow, how had that happened?

His chest rose and fell as he blew out a breath. "No condoms, Ellie. Best I go to my own room."

"Max Brannigan, you're an adorable idiot," she said, rolling over and yanking open her bedside table. When she found the box of condoms, she took them out and threw them at him. "I'd really like you to stay."

He caught them, his eyes widening in surprise.

"A girl should always be prepared. I've had those for about three years now, but they aren't expired for another two years, so there."

He arched an eyebrow. "So you've known the date on these condoms for the past three years?"

She dropped her gaze as fresh heat rolled through her. "No. I checked them a couple of days ago."

"A couple of days—" His voice choked off and he ripped the box open and took out a strip, tearing one off and handing it to her. The rest he laid on the bedside table. Then he kicked out of his jeans. He was wearing black briefs with a white band, heaven help her, and his cock bulged up and to the left. The tip poked out of the top of his briefs, and Ellie swallowed. When he pushed the briefs off, she nearly moaned in anticipation.

"Put it on me," he told her, and she tore the package open. When she reached for him, he was hot and hard and smooth. He wasn't small either. The little groan that issued from his throat when she rolled the condom on gratified her.

She already knew what he did to her. It was nice to know she could do something in return.

He came down on top of her, yet he was careful not to crush her into the mattress. Instinctively, she lifted her legs and wrapped them around his hips. And then she felt him, so big and hard, and a little current of panic washed through her.

It had been a long time, and she didn't know how this was going to feel. Not really. She hoped, sure. But what if it was awful? What if he was too big and it had been too long and it hurt?

"Ellie."

She snapped her gaze to his.

Gray eyes studied her solemnly. "Breathe, honey."

"I am breathing." Her voice was small, tight, as if she were holding her breath.

He held himself up on his elbows, his thumbs glided along her cheeks, and he smiled softly. "Not going to hurt you. It'll be good, I promise."

Impossibly, she believed him. "I know."

He pressed inside her then, his body invading hers, filling her so full she thought she couldn't possibly take another inch. And then he was there, deep inside her, and her fear subsided. He moved slowly, carefully, and her passion came to life again, her body responding, opening. If she'd felt good before, she felt even better now.

He kissed her, and the world melted away. There was nothing in this bed, nothing between them but skin and heat and passion. It didn't take long for the spark to flare again, and she found herself rising to meet him, pushing her hips up to his as every nerve ending in her body raced toward fulfillment. He moved faster then, harder, and the flame rose higher.

She felt as if she were flying, as if her entire life depended on what happened between them right now. The tension inside her wound tighter than before, so impossibly tight that she thought surely she would explode when it snapped this time.

And then it broke in two and she couldn't breathe as her body dissolved into one long wave of intense pleasure. It rolled over her and through her, and she cried out, gripping his shoulders with her fingers and his waist with her legs.

He didn't stop moving, didn't stop driving her higher and higher, so impossibly high that she thought she'd never come down. With a last hard thrust and a groan, he spilled himself into her, his body quivering as his release crashed over him.

She didn't quite know what to expect as they floated back to earth. She didn't do casual sex, not usually, but she certainly had tonight.

And, oh God, she'd do it again in a heartbeat if he wanted to. Which was dangerous and stupid and the epitome of a bad idea, if she was honest with herself.

Max Brannigan already owned her farm. Now he might just own a little piece of her heart.

CHAPTER FOURTEEN

Max had died and gone to heaven. He was buried deep inside a beautiful woman who still trembled with the force of her orgasm, and he'd just had a pretty amazing release himself.

He hated to move, but he had to. He kissed Ellie softly as she arched into him and kissed him back eagerly, then he rolled off her and went to deal with the condom. He looked at himself in the mirror and frowned at what he saw. He was naked and satisfied, but at what price had he taken that satisfaction?

Ellie was a hardworking, decent person who didn't need his kind of shit in her life. If he was honest with himself, he knew he wasn't going to force her to sell. He'd give her time, and then he'd sell the farm when he had the authority to do so.

He'd even give her half the profit, though James would yell he was a fool, no matter if her year was up. Because she needed it if she was going to keep breeding and training horses somewhere else.

So if he knew that, what was he still doing here? He could call Ian back, take the offer to fight in Acamar, and be on a plane out of the US by the day after tomorrow.

But a part of him rebelled at the thought. That was the part that wanted to go back into Ellie's bedroom, climb into bed with her, and hold her all night. And keep holding her every night from now on, at least until this flame between them flickered and died.

He didn't know what he was going to do in the long run, but he could do what he wanted for tonight anyway.

He walked back into her bedroom, uncertain what he might find. Would Ellie be covered up to her chin with the sheet, or would she still be lying naked and exposed in the rumpled bed? Would she want him to get out, or would she want him to stay?

She was lying on her side, her eyes closed, her knees curled up tight. He'd nearly forgotten how tired she was, and his chest ached at the sight of her. Was that tenderness he felt?

The covers were a mess—and she still wore the black bra he'd never fully removed. He glanced around her bedroom, taking it in for the first time since he'd carried her in here. It wasn't frilly or girly like he might have expected, but plain and neat. Her covers were white, her sheets were white, and her curtains were a pale blue. Her furniture consisted of a bed, a dresser with a mirror, and two night tables. There was a blue chair in one corner and precisely six pictures on all four walls.

It was no surprise the pictures were of horses. There was a faded ribbon hanging on one wall, along with a photo of a horse and rider, and he went over to read what it said. First place, Kentucky State Fair, World's Championship Horse Show. But it was dated 1980, which meant it couldn't be hers. Her mother's, most likely.

A wave of tenderness rolled through him at the thought of Ellie preserving this memento in her own room when she had a whole house to do so in. She was complicated and sweet and fierce, and he realized in that moment that he admired her very much.

She didn't quit when many would. When the odds were stacked against her, she kept on going. It's what a warrior did, truth be told. And Ellie was definitely a warrior.

"Max," she murmured, and he turned and went to her side. He climbed into bed beside her and indulged his desire to pull her into his arms. He also unsnapped the bra and gently tugged it free, dropping it over the side of the bed.

Ellie was warm and naked in his embrace, and his dick started to harden again.

She snuggled up to him, pressing her cheek to his chest, and sighed. "Sleepy," she said. "Sorry."

He stroked her hair and then kissed her forehead. "Sleep then. I'll be here when you wake."

"Promise?"

"Yeah, I promise."

At least this time he would be. But not for much longer.

Waking naked in bed with a man was a new sensation for her. Or an old sensation she'd forgotten that was suddenly new again. She and Dave had never actually lived together, and the nights they spent with each other were typically at his place. He'd stayed here too, but not as often. Momma hadn't said anything, but Ellie always felt strange having her boyfriend in her room in the same house as her mother.

At first she didn't want to move for fear of waking Max, but when she glanced up into his face, his eyes burned as they stared back at her.

"Morning, Ellie."

"Morning."

Now what?

Thank you for the amazing orgasms last night, or *Hey, that sex stuff rocked the house—can we do it again?*

She settled for running a hand down his bare side, over his hip, and around to cup his firm ass. Lord have mercy, what a fine behind it was too.

His cock jumped, and she sucked in a breath at the evidence he was already hard. She threw a leg over his hip and brought herself closer. Just so there'd be no doubt what she wanted right then.

He growled a little as he cupped her breast and dipped his head to take her nipple between his teeth. Her fingers curled into his skin as lightning streaked through her.

She'd thought maybe last night was a fluke, a one-off, but her body didn't seem to think so at all.

He reached behind her and grabbed the foil packets. She took them from him and tore one free, sheathing him as quickly as she could manage. He flipped onto his back and let her take control, which surprised her, but then as she positioned herself and sank down on him, she was glad he'd done so.

She was a little bit sore. Okay, maybe a lot sore. In a good way, of course, but if he'd been the one in charge... Well, it might be a little unbearable until she found her rhythm.

But Max knew, somehow, and he let her be the one to set the pace. He gripped her hips and his eyes flashed fire as she rose and fell, rose and fell. She moved slowly and he didn't try to make her go faster.

And then he reached down and found her clit, flicking it with his thumb, and a shiver snaked up her spine and down into her toes as she gasped.

"I think you like that," he murmured.

"Don't know what gave you that idea." Her nipples were tight little points, and the pressure gathering in her core made her move a little faster.

"You're beautiful, Ellie. So fucking sexy."

He lifted himself off the bed and sucked a nipple into his mouth. His thumb didn't stop and the pressure inside her grew until she had to move faster to keep pace with it.

"I don't want to come yet," she gasped—but it was too late. Her release tore through her, rippling from her core out into her toes and fingers, making her moan and gasp as she rode him frantically to the very end.

When she would have collapsed on him, he stroked into her harder and faster—and the fire ignited again. He took her over the edge once more, thrusting up inside her as she clung to him helplessly, and then he followed her into beautiful oblivion.

She was panting, but so was he. She pushed off him and onto her back, letting the air cool her. He got up and went to the bathroom. When he returned, she took a moment to admire the long, beautiful lines of his body. She thought he might crawl between the sheets again, and she looked forward to lying against him and feeling his skin next to hers.

But he reached for his clothes instead. "Horses to take care of, babe," he said when she would have protested.

She picked up her phone and looked at the time. A quarter past six. "Holy shit!"

She jumped from the bed and fumbled for her clothing, and Max laughed softly. "Relax, I heard Miguel's truck almost an hour ago."

She was hopping on one foot, trying to tug on her panties and failing miserably. She stopped and gaped at the sexy man in her bedroom. "You heard him? And you didn't wake me?"

"You needed sleep, Ellie. You've had some long days lately. Miguel can handle feeding horses."

She wanted to argue, but he was right. Miguel *could* handle it, and though she felt guilty she'd let him feed alone, there were mornings when they each had to take up the slack for the other. She hadn't been sick in over a year, but the last time when she'd gotten the stomach flu and went down for a week... Well, that had been bad. Poor Miguel, and poor Lacey.

And poor Ellie, because without lessons that week, she'd lost money.

"I still need to get down there and help."

Max came over and took her by the shoulders. "I know. But how about you take a moment for coffee and some breakfast first?"

She loved the way his hands rested on her shoulders and the way warmth flowed through her because of it. She could get used to this…

No.

Because he wasn't staying. He'd already said so.

"Are you fixing the coffee?" she asked.

He grinned. "Yeah, I'll fix it. And breakfast too."

"I'm fresh out of Pop-Tarts," she teased.

"Woman," he growled. "I can do better than that. How's toast?"

"Oh, *so* hard," she said.

He lifted an eyebrow. "You still referring to the toast?"

Flirty? She did *not* do this kind of thing. Until now. Until Max. "Unless you've got something else for me."

"I've definitely got something else for you, Ellie. You just let me know when you want it."

"As much as I'd like to say right now, I think it'll have to wait until tonight. But I definitely want it."

He backed away from her, his clothes held casually in a fist, his penis more than half hard. So, so beautiful. She could stare at him for hours. Maybe she'd ask him to take his clothes off tonight and just wander around the house that way…

"Get your ass dressed and get downstairs," he told her. "Breakfast and coffee. Then we work."

He disappeared through the door, and she had to stand there and just breathe for a few seconds. Max Brannigan had spent the night in her bed. In *her* bed. She was in so much trouble… and she couldn't wait to tell Lacey all about it.

When Ellie came down for coffee, Max had fixed toast *and* eggs. Because he knew how to take care of himself and cooking was, while not one of his best skills, *a* skill.

Ellie looked beautiful, but when didn't she? She'd pulled her hair into a ponytail, and she wore what he now knew were her work jodhpurs and a T-shirt. She smiled as she came into the kitchen, and he thought he could see that smile every morning for a good long while yet.

A dangerous thought, but there it was.

"You made eggs."

"Never said I couldn't cook, babe. You assumed."

She picked up her plate and started to eat where she stood. He knew her well enough to know she never slowed down, and when she thought she was late to the barn… Well, she wasn't slowing down for sure.

"Mmm, these are good."

"Better than Pop-Tarts?"

"Definitely."

"You have lessons today?"

"One at ten, yes. And I have to work Champ this morning. There's a show next weekend in Tennessee that I plan to take him to."

Her sunny disposition seemed to cloud up for a second. Max wanted to know why. "Is that a bad thing?"

"No, not at all—but it's his debut, and so I worry a little bit."

She seemed like she worried a lot, but he didn't push her. "I'm sure he'll be spectacular."

She nibbled her lip and a shot of pure desire went straight to his groin.

"I have so much depending on this, Max. I know what I'm doing—but the ring is a special place. You can do everything right every single day. And then you go in there and it all falls apart because you're nervous and you communicate that to the horse. Or maybe he's having a bad day. A kid jumps on the bleachers just as you go by and he breaks stride—right in front of the judge. So many variables."

"Every person in the ring has the same variables, right?"

She nodded and set her plate down, finished with the eggs. She picked up a piece of toast. "They do."

"Then nothing you can do except your very best. It's the same for all of us, Ellie. Let your training take over. Do the job and let everything else fall away for those few minutes."

"You're right."

"I know I am." Because for him, it was a matter of life and death sometimes. Oftentimes.

He handed her the go-cup of coffee he'd made and captured her lips in a kiss. "Get down to the barn and help Miguel before you explode."

Her fingers wrapped around his where they held the cup as she kissed him back. "I could get used to this," she said softly. "Breakfast and coffee, I mean. And hot sex. Definitely that."

He laughed. "You're babbling, Ellie."

"I am, aren't I?"

"Don't worry, I knew what you meant. Neither one of us is talking about picket fences here."

"Picket fences are for amateurs," she said, laughing. And then she went out the door and down the steps, walking across the field toward the barn. He went over to the window and watched her. She strode with purpose and determination. She pulled her phone out of her pocket and put it to her ear. A second later, his phone buzzed. He'd given her the number a few days ago when they'd been dealing with Lacey and the restraining order.

"Miss me already?" he asked and then wanted to kick himself for it. Why was he flirting with her? Carrying this any further than it had already gone? Sex was one thing, but flirty fun that hinted at emotions was quite another.

"Maybe," she said, and warmth flowed through him. Dammit. "I forgot to tell you that the books are in my office. Down the hall from the kitchen, third door on the left. You'll find it. They're in the top right-hand drawer. They aren't exciting, but everything is there."

He felt like an asshole all of a sudden. "It can wait until you're ready to go over it with me."

"It's okay, Max. Have a look. I'll answer any questions you might have. The picture isn't exciting, I'll just tell you that. But we're making do."

"You're doing a good job, Ellie. I know that." And he did know it, even if he thought she'd be better off with racehorses. But that wasn't the hand she'd been dealt nor the one he'd inherited.

"Day at a time," she said. "It's all we can do. Okay, gotta go. Walking into the barn now."

She ended the call, and he put his phone in his pocket. Then he stood there and looked out at the barn in the early-morning light. The horses in the field were munching hay happily, and the baby he'd watched being born frolicked in the dew while his mother ate.

161

Peaceful. So damned pretty. He hadn't expected to appreciate quiet mornings in Kentucky, but he was learning that he did. Very much.

He especially appreciated them when he woke up with a beautiful woman and then made love to her before ever leaving the bed. *That* was how to start a day, no matter where you were.

Max cleaned up the dishes, drying them and putting them in the cabinets before he hung up the towel and went to find the office. It was a room with bay windows, bookshelves, and more old carpeting that needed ripping out. There were photos on the walls of horses and riders getting ribbons at various shows. The entire history of Applegate Farm was on these walls, he realized as he walked around the room. There were photos in the barn too, along one wall, but no ribbons.

He picked up a photo on a table. A woman who looked remarkably like Ellie, but wasn't, stared back at him. It was the same woman from the photo his mother was in. Pamela Applegate. She sat on a big horse, her smile wide, and a man and woman stood beside her. One held a ribbon and the other held a silver trophy.

There were a lot of pictures like that. There were photos of Ellie on horses, and even older photos he assumed were her grandparents. Yeah, the Applegates had quite the history.

Max put down the photo he'd picked up and went over to the desk. The account books were where she'd said they would be. He opened the page and ran his eye over what was written there. Why wasn't she doing this on a computer? The ancient-looking PC sitting quietly on the desk told him the probable answer.

He ran down the columns. Feed, shoeing, utilities, maintenance, vet bills, show fees, Miguel's pay. There was a payment on a tractor too. They paid workers to help haul hay when they harvested, but that wasn't a big expenditure.

The incoming column wasn't as long as the outgoing. Seven horses that didn't belong to Ellie were boarded on the farm, and their monthly fees added something to the coffers but not a lot. Lessons were a big part of her income. The training column was anemic, though five of the seven horses added a small amount there. He flipped the pages and went back five years. He did a double take. The training column was enormous then. So enormous that he frowned. What the hell had happened to change that?

He flipped inward, following the money. About three years ago, everything slowed to a moderate flow. Miguel had told him that Ellie's mother had started acting erratically and chased off most of their clients. Six months after that, the revenue squeezed even more—and then there was an influx of cash.

His father. Pamela had gone to his father, and Colin had loaned her money. Where had that money gone? He frowned as he went over the columns month by month. Some of it had gone to the farm, but not the majority. There was no accounting for that kind of money—

It hit him suddenly where the money went. Pamela's medical bills. Her treatment. Holy shit. He hadn't thought of that at first, hadn't thought that the money the Applegates borrowed went to anything but the farm. He'd thought she'd had medical insurance, and he'd never considered they'd spent money on her treatment.

163

Had his father known? It made him ill to think his father would have taken the deed to the farm in exchange for money to keep Ellie's mother alive. And then he rejected that idea outright. Dad had been a lot of things—a hard-nosed businessman for sure, but not ruthless. Not *so* ruthless he'd take the deed to a dying woman's property in exchange for helping her get treatment.

He had to call Aunt Claire. Except it was three thirty in the morning in California, and she wouldn't appreciate a call right now.

He closed the ledger and sat there frowning for a long while. Dad had given him a horse farm in Kentucky. A horse farm with a gorgeous, hardworking woman who was determined to save her heritage. Ellie Applegate worked her ass off to keep the farm she loved, but she wasn't working to repay a mortgage so much as she was working to repay medical bills. Did that change the reality of their situation? Did it change *him?*

Max felt his jaw crack. Goddammit—maybe it did. And he didn't know what he was going to do about it.

CHAPTER FIFTEEN

Champ worked like, well, a champ. Ellie patted his steaming chestnut neck as she brought him to a halt in the center of the arena. She knew how her mother must have felt when she'd ridden Applegate champions in the days of old. They hadn't had a champion like Champ before though. Ellie had been cheeky when she'd named him Champ as a newborn, but dammit, they needed a self-fulfilling prophecy for a change.

She'd bet money on the fact he was the best they'd ever had. Momma had trained some excellent horses, and so had Gramps. They'd won a world's championship once for themselves, and they'd trained world's champions for others. They'd had reserve world's champions and clients who'd paid good money to have Applegate horses.

They'd never had a horse like Champ before—a horse that could possibly be a world's grand champion someday. Or maybe she was deluded. Maybe she'd pinned all her hopes and dreams on him to the point she couldn't see reality anymore.

Momma had bred him, but Ellie had trained him. Momma would have, but she'd gotten sick. Out of necessity, the task had fallen to Ellie. She'd used everything she'd learned from Momma, and she'd done the best job she knew how to do. She had a horse who could fly at the rack, who had natural high action, and who never tired of performing. He arched his neck, flagged his tail, and strutted his stuff without hesitation. She couldn't ask for a better horse.

But was it enough? She didn't have the deep pockets of the big farms. It was everything she could do to scrape together the entry fees. She had three clients who planned to show next weekend, and that helped her with the gas and the fees somewhat. But she had to stay in the barn instead of a hotel. The stall fees were cheaper than a hotel room, and there were showers in the restrooms at the showgrounds. She had her cot and her sleeping bag, and it wasn't anything new for her.

In the old days, Momma had sometimes stayed near the horses when some trainers were unscrupulous enough to attempt to upset a horse's performance by giving them sedatives or, worse, making them come up lame.

She didn't think anyone was going to harm Champ, but if she was honest with herself, it wasn't a risk she was willing to take. People were capable of anything when big money was on the line.

Not that it would be next weekend. This was only a preliminary, but it was the first time anyone would see Champ work in public—which was also why it was so critical that he do well. He might totally wig out. She knew that. He might get to the ring and have a meltdown, though she thought she knew him better than that.

He was sensible and he was all business under saddle. But he was still a stallion, and he was young. Put him in an environment with lots of horses, many of them mares—some possibly in season—and lights, sounds, and smells unlike what he was used to, and he could have a complete and total breakdown.

She just had to hope he didn't. That training and the desire to perform would take over and he'd be brilliant. It was critical that he be brilliant.

She dismounted and took Champ into the barn, putting him in the crossties and unsaddling. Then she rubbed him down and put a cooler on him since the mornings could still be a little chilly.

"Morning," Lacey called out as she walked up with an extra coffee. And then her expression changed, her eyes widening slightly as she gazed at Ellie. She thrust the coffee out. "Girl, you had better tell me everything!"

Ellie's heart skipped. Now was her chance—but could she say any of it? Or was it too private? She laughed as she took the insulated cup. "That obvious?"

"Something is obvious, yes indeed. What happened?"

Ellie sipped the hot coffee. It didn't help that she thought of Max fixing her a cup earlier. She hadn't seen him since she'd left the house, but of course she'd thought of him. And every damned moment that had happened between the time he'd picked her up on the porch and the time she'd gotten dressed this morning. She didn't remember ever feeling that, well, *sexually satisfied* before.

"A lot happened, Lacey. I… Well, the long dry spell is over, let's put it that way."

Lacey squealed like a teenager. "I want to know *all* the details. Is he amazing? Hung? Does he know what to do with all that handsomeness or what?"

Ellie shook her head and laughed. "Dear God, are we sixteen or what?"

"Puh-leeze. Neither one of us knew what the hell sex was at sixteen."

"Fine, true. We were late bloomers in the scheme of things."

"And?"

"And he knows what he's doing. I've never, ever been so... thoroughly worn out from spending the night with a man. Yes, he's amazing. And blessed in that, er, department."

"Oh, I'm so jealous." Lacey sighed and then hurried to correct herself. "Not because of Max," she said. "Just because you're getting some and I'm not."

Ellie snorted. "I haven't gotten *any*, as you put it, for over two years. I think I'm due."

"You are definitely due. So what now?"

Ellie frowned and leaned back against the wall. "I have no idea."

"Do you think he still wants to sell? Or will he change his mind?"

"We had sex, Lacey. We aren't getting married. Of course he still wants to sell. This changes nothing."

Lacey's eyes flashed. "Then honey, you have *got* to get in there and screw his brains out. Make him crazy. Don't let him figure out which way is up or which way is down. You've got this."

Ellie laughed. "Lacey, I love you. But you give me far more credit than I deserve."

Lacey shook her head. "You have no idea, do you? You are gorgeous and smart and so, so interesting. He's crazy for you, even if he doesn't quite understand why. This is when you go in for the kill. Hammer it home, ha-ha, and don't let him think about anything but you. Now is not the time to be timid."

Ellie couldn't help but gape at her friend. "He is *not* crazy for me. You're deluded. He's been here five days. That's not enough time to be crazy about anything."

"Ellie, I say this with love—you're an idiot. There's definitely something there, and it's your job to make sure he knows it."

"*I* don't know it. How can I make sure he knows something I don't?" She wanted to throw up her hands and shout her frustration, but Lacey frowned at her like she was stupid.

"Honey, please. You have known this man for *five days* and you have apparently spent the entire night doing the nasty with him. You wouldn't do that—have *not* done that—with anyone else in so short a time, and you know it."

Ellie felt herself coloring. "I haven't had a chance. Who else is there?"

"Seriously? You've had opportunities. What about Jack, the Thoroughbred trainer over at Sunset Farms? He came around here for weeks, and he doesn't know diddly about saddlebreds. Then there was Brad, the insurance agent who helped you file that claim after the wind storm. And Peter, the single father who brought his daughter out for lessons last year."

Ellie felt as if she were burning up from the inside out. Okay, so there'd been a few men who had shown interest. She hadn't been interested in any of them. That was not a crime. Max was the first one to move into her place, and that had to be what made the difference. He was here twenty-four seven—except he hadn't been here all the time, had he? Those few days after Lacey had filed the restraining order, he'd hardly been around. Ellie didn't know why that was, but she'd noticed.

"You're exaggerating," she said. It was a lame excuse, and they both knew it.

"Whatever. Seriously, you have got to ride that pony for all it's worth. You didn't cross that line because you were tired or bored or horny. You crossed it because there's something about *him* that you like very much."

Ellie dropped her head in defeat. "God, don't say that Lacey. I do like him—but he's not staying. I heard him on the phone last night. He's got a job waiting in the desert, wherever that is, and he'll go there soon. He's told me he has nothing to give me but his body, so there's no point in expecting more."

Lacey frowned. Hard. "Elinor Caroline Applegate, I am shocked at you. Since when do you give up on anything? Since when do you let *anyone* tell you what they will and will not do where you are concerned? You aren't a quitter, and you never have been. If you were, Champ wouldn't be the horse he is today. Applegate Farm would have folded when your mother died. And God knows what would have happened to me, because I'd have let Brice browbeat me into believing I was worthless and stupid if I hadn't had you to turn to."

Ellie's insides squeezed tight. Her eyes felt gritty and raw as she swallowed back hot tears. Not because she felt hopeless over a man, but because her best friend in the world knew her so well. "I would do anything for you, Lacey. You know that. You are not worthless or stupid or any other damned negative thing Brice tried to beat you down with."

Lacey's smile trembled at the corners. "I know that, El. If I didn't, I wouldn't be saying this, would I? And you are worth so much *more* than a man who says he has nothing more to give than his body. Seriously, you go up there and you fight for that shit. Fight for what you're worth and what you want."

Ellie shook her head sadly. "It's okay, sweetie. I know what I'm worth—but that doesn't mean Max is going to stay, or that I want him to stay. It's sex. Good sex, sure, but you said it yourself. Five days is all we've spent together—I'm not in love with him. And he is definitely not in love with me."

Lacey's frown grew more fierce. "Then you need to work harder, don't you?"

"Lacey, I—"

But Max walked around the corner of the barn just then, and Ellie's tongue grew thick in her mouth. He strode up to them as if he hadn't a care in the world, but his expression was at odds with his body language. He looked... tense.

"Max," Lacey said, smiling like the minx she was.

"Hey, Lacey." Max went over and gave her a quick squeeze. Ellie wasn't jealous, because she knew there was nothing between them, but she was definitely envious that he felt so at ease with Lacey he could hug her without a thought. Lacey lifted an eyebrow at Ellie. She wanted to laugh, and she wanted to pinch her friend at the same time. Horrible tease.

"Everything okay? No Brice the asshole?" he asked.

Lacey smiled. "Nope, no Brice. Whatever you said to him on the sidewalk scared him good. That and the restraining order. I owe you. Free haircuts forever?"

Max laughed. "How about free haircuts for now? Though I'm happy to pay you."

"You don't want free haircuts for life? You aren't planning to leave us, are you?"

Ellie wanted to kick Lacey in her backside, but Lacey just smiled and acted all innocent as she batted her eyelashes at Max.

Max's gaze flickered to Ellie. She felt the heat of his gaze like a torch, whether he intended it or not. Her nerve endings prickled to life.

"I'm not leaving right now."

"But you *are* leaving." Lacey was pushing for an answer. Ellie wanted to clap her hand over Lacey's mouth— and she wanted to know the answer too.

"Eventually," Max said. Which was as much of a non-answer as it was possible to give.

He'd asked her last night if she'd wanted him to go. She'd said yes. And then she'd said no. She'd been confused for so many reasons when she'd said those things, but the idea of him leaving now made her heart cry out. Which was ridiculous, because he'd been here five days. *Five days.*

"Well," Lacey said, straightening. "I have to go and get Clover ready for our ride."

She strode away and left them alone. Ellie's mouth went dry. She'd spent the night in this man's arms, but now she didn't know what to say. Or what to do. She was glad she had a coffee cup to hold on to, because otherwise she'd be tempted to put her hands on him.

Max threw a glance toward Lacey's retreating back and then turned to Ellie. He was grinning, and that made her heart skip a beat. "Subtle, isn't she?"

Ellie shrugged. "As a match in a fireworks store."

"You told her."

Ellie blushed bright red. She could feel it, but she hoped he chalked it up to the exertion of riding Champ. "I didn't have to. She knows me well. Apparently my face gives it away."

Max laughed. "You do look pretty satisfied."

And just like that, her insides melted into a hot, gooey puddle of desire. "Thanks again for that."

He came over and took the coffee cup from her. Or, more accurately, he unfolded her arms and widened them so he could put his around her waist and tug her in close. She held the cup against his arm and tried not to tremble.

"Anytime, babe."

"Anytime until you leave, you mean." Now why had she said that?

"I thought you wanted me to go." His voice was warm and slightly mocking. But there was humor in it.

"Maybe I like having you around. You're useful."

He snorted. "Free labor, *you* mean." His voice dropped an octave. "Or do you mean useful in bed?"

"All the above, Max. Stick around long enough, and you'll renovate my entire house. I'll pay you in orgasms. It's the perfect exchange."

He dipped his head until he could nibble the skin of her neck. She couldn't help the sigh that escaped.

"I'm not going to disagree with that," he said.

"So you're staying?" Was she really asking that? After everything?

"I'm staying for now, babe." He sighed and straightened. "I looked at the books."

Her insides squeezed for a different reason. Now he knew how bad it was. How little the farm brought in. If she sold a horse, then that floated her for a while. Board and training paid the monthly expenses, but little else. Not that she thought she could fool him into thinking the farm was profitable. She'd never thought that.

But it could be. It had been once. She could make it so again. She just needed *time*.

"What do you want to know?"

Champ had turned his head and was nibbling the chain of a crosstie. Silly beast. Her heart filled with love for him, and then sadness followed. Because he was the one thing she had to sell to keep everything else.

"You didn't tell me that the money your mother borrowed went to medical bills."

Ellie blinked. She hadn't told him about her mother—but Miguel could have, or Lacey. Or anyone in town. It wasn't a secret what had happened to Pamela Applegate.

She stepped out of his embrace and over to Champ to gently pry the chain from his mouth. Then she kissed his soft nose. Just because. When she turned around again, Max was waiting. Looking intense and concerned.

"You probably know she had a brain tumor," Ellie began. "She wasn't diagnosed for so long." She swallowed, the hurt as fresh now as it had been then. "But it wouldn't have mattered, according to the doctors. What she had was fast-moving and irreversible. Even if they'd operated, it wouldn't have changed the outcome. Maybe given her a little more time."

"I'm sorry, Ellie. I truly am."

"I know you are." She sucked in a breath. "It was only little things at first. She'd get violently angry out of nowhere. Cuss and throw things and be so, so mean. And then she'd cry and apologize and everything would be fine for a few days. Then back to the volatile Pam. She was so unpredictable that all our clients left. A few tried to stick it out, but she insulted them one by one—it was ugly, Max. I begged her to stop, begged them not to go. But it was too late. They left us, and we suddenly had nothing. She called your father in one of her more lucid moments. I don't know what she said to him, but he gave her the money. She went to a new doctor, got new tests—and they found it. The money your father gave us paid the expenses of the farm for months—but the bulk of it went to her care. She needed full-time caregivers for a while—and then she was in hospice at the end."

Ellie took a shaky sip of her coffee. She hated remembering the gaunt, frightened woman her mother became. She hated remembering the anger and yelling, even though it hadn't been Momma's fault.

Max came over and pulled her into his arms. He held her close, just held her, and she closed her eyes and laid her cheek against his chest. His heartbeat was strong and steady, and she took comfort in it. In him.

Oh God, he was starting to mean too much to her. It hit her as she stood there in his arms and wanted to let him take care of her troubles that she was in too deep. Too soon, too deep. Was she that pitiful that she couldn't stand on her own two feet when a man showed her compassion?

Carefully, she extracted herself. She gave him a smile, though it wavered at the corners. "That's the story then. That's where the money went."

He was frowning. "We're going to figure this out, Ellie. I don't want you to lose the farm. I don't want to take it away from you."

Tears pressed against the backs of her eyes. "But you want to start your business and change what you do with your life. That's important too."

Had she really just said that? Of course she had, because while she was singularly focused on keeping the farm, she also cared what happened to him. She hadn't meant to, hadn't wanted to—but it was so much more complicated than a Brannigan rich boy coming to take her farm away, wasn't it? For him, it meant a new start where he might not be in as much danger as the kind of jobs he did now. And that was important to her. Because she cared.

He gave her a lopsided grin that stole her heart. "Yeah, well, I can wait a while longer. Been waiting this long— what's the difference?"

"I don't want you to sacrifice what you want so I can have what I want. It's not right."

"It's the way the world works sometimes, Ellie."

"Hey, we're ready to go if you are," Lacey called out. She was standing in the aisle with Clover, and Ellie realized her friend must have cross-tied the mare in her stall instead of bringing her out here where they'd interrupt the conversation. Lacey had probably taken as much time as she could manage, but she needed to ride and get to work, and she needed Ellie to instruct her.

Ellie gave Max a look. She didn't know what she wanted to say to him, what made sense.

"Go," he said. "We can talk later."

She started down the aisle toward Lacey. "I'm coming."

CHAPTER SIXTEEN

He'd said they could talk later, but instead he had Ellie bent over the edge of her bed, stroking into her from behind while she fisted the covers and shoved her hips backward, taking him in so deep that he thought he'd lose his mind.

She was fire, this woman. Fire and heat, and she inspired feelings he hadn't ever had before. He didn't know what they meant, but he knew they felt damn good. Being inside Ellie was one of the best things in his life right now.

He tried to make it last, but there was no way that was happening as good as this felt. He came in a hot, hard, gasping rush. She tightened around him and cried out as her own release slammed into her.

They collapsed on the bed, his face buried in her hair, the heat of their bodies mingling as he pushed her hair aside and nuzzled her neck.

"Sorry," he said. "I meant to feed you first."

She laughed. "I prefer this. We can eat later."

He slid from her body and went to deal with the condom, then returned and gathered her into his arms. They lay naked on the bed, the covers thrown back, the ceiling fan gliding lazily around and around.

"I planned to take you to Malone's."

"You still can. I could use a steak tonight."

He'd worked in the house today, slicing open painted-shut windows, assessing the floors in all the rooms—there was still plenty of carpeting that needed to be ripped out—and sizing up the walls. This house had a ton of potential. Renovated, it could be one of those showplaces in *Southern Living* or *Architectural Digest*. There was a long way to go to that caliber, but the bones were there and he got a little lost in thinking about it.

He'd gone up to take a shower after sanding the walls in the hall—and when he came out, the door to Ellie's bedroom had been open. She'd been standing there, tugging her T-shirt over her head, and he'd gone from zero to sixty in about half a second.

He'd restrained himself though. She'd been planning to hit the shower—so he hit it with her, no matter that he'd just showered. What they'd begun in the shower, they'd finished just now on her bed. It was, quite simply, heaven. How the fuck was he supposed to walk away from this?

But he had to. He thought of his brothers—Luke, Gabe, Hunter, and Knox—and the way they'd succumbed to what they thought was love.

He knew better. He knew Ellie was special, and he knew he cared about her. But it wasn't love. It was lust. Pure, simple, unadulterated lust. He could burn himself out in the heat of her body and walk away free.

And he *would* do that. Yes, he would. Soon.

Reluctantly, he got up and tugged her to her feet. The late afternoon light slanted in through the blinds in her room and bathed her body in golden rays. She was soft in all the right places and leanly muscled too. He could spend hours exploring her.

"Let's go to dinner," he said, "and you can tell me what happened in the barn today."

She arched an eyebrow. "You don't really want to hear all that."

"I do. Really." When she still looked at him with disbelief, he ran his hands up and down her arms. "It's interesting to me. I swear."

He left her to get dressed as he grabbed his towel and went downstairs to his own room. He quickly changed into jeans and a T-shirt, ran his hand through his hair, and he was done. His phone rang and he picked it up. He smiled when he saw who it was.

"Aunt Claire," he said when he answered.

"Maxie, it's good to hear your voice."

He didn't let many people get away with calling him Maxie, but Aunt Claire was one of them. Hell, probably the only one he let get away with it, come to think of it. His brothers only called him that when they wanted to irritate him.

"How's California these days?" He hadn't been out there in so long, but he was sure it was the same. Best Mexican food anywhere, which he sometimes missed like crazy. He'd had burritos on the East Coast, but they weren't anywhere as good as a real California burrito.

"Sunny. Glorious," she said. "So how are you doing in Kentucky, honey?"

"Fine. It's pretty. So green and lush compared to back home in Calabasas." Not that DC wasn't green and lush too, but he didn't spend a lot of time there. Most of his time was spent in the deserts of the Middle East these days, though he'd done assignments in other locations too.

"Thanks for that picture of Kathleen and Pam. I loved it." She paused for a second before she kept speaking, and he could picture her face screwing up as she thought about what she wanted to say. "I didn't realize your father had bought Applegate Farm. I haven't thought about that place in years, quite honestly. But I remember it was so pretty. Pam and her parents were terrific, and your mother spent a lot of time there. She loved horses."

His heart pinched. "I didn't know that growing up. Wish I had. Why didn't she have horses at the ranch? We had the space. Even had barns."

"I think she always intended to get a horse or two, but life was so busy with you boys and she kept putting off. She didn't think it was fair to the animals, I imagine."

"Mary Lou sends her regards, by the way," he said, and Aunt Claire laughed.

"Oh my goodness, is she still there? Still has that diner in town?"

"Yes. Amazing food too."

"How is Pam these days?"

Max felt himself frowning as he thought of Ellie's face that morning in the barn as she described her mother's sickness. "She died about two years ago. Brain tumor."

"Oh my goodness. I didn't know."

He could hear the emotion in her voice. That was Aunt Claire—soft and sweet and caring. Without her as the main

181

female influence in their lives after their mother died, he didn't know how he and his brothers would have turned out.

"Her daughter runs the farm now. I think most of the money Pam borrowed from Dad went to palliative care."

"Oh dear. But I don't think he knew that. He would have mentioned it. Pam and I weren't close, but he knew that I knew her too."

"Yeah, I'm sure he would have said something." Pam Applegate had borrowed money to keep her farm afloat and then needed it to ease her pain and offer her some comfort while she was dying. Or maybe she'd thought she could be cured. He didn't know. Still, it wasn't quite the same as mismanaging money and needing a bailout.

"He had to have known she died. I wonder why he didn't tell me then?"

"Her daughter kept paying the loan as scheduled. He probably didn't realize it for quite some time. You know Dad—always too busy to know whether he was coming or going."

"Yes, you're right. He may have only found out about Pam when he got sick and started writing his bequests. If he wouldn't tell me he was dying, he certainly wasn't going to tell me about anyone else's death at that point."

"That sounds about right." Max tried not to feel a pinch of anger at the thought of his dad moving to the Bahamas and telling no one he was ill—but it didn't quite work. He was still pissed that no one had known. That Dad had chosen to spend the past few weeks of his life alone.

He could hear Aunt Claire fiddling with the beads around her neck, and he knew she was thinking about something. "Your father left you the farm because he thought it would do something for you. I don't know what. It's clear he left the gifts he did to you and your brothers for specific reasons. Only you can find that reason, Maxie."

He had to agree. The idea that Dad had randomly gifted him with a horse farm in Kentucky was no longer a possibility in his mind. Max had inherited Applegate Farm for what? To meet Ellie? That didn't make sense, because Ellie and Dad had never met—besides, the idea of Dad playing matchmaker from the grave wasn't quite right. Or not in his case anyway. In the case of Luke and Lizzie, where they'd had a past and clearly belonged together, Max could see it.

So what else was there? Did Dad think he needed to learn about horses and patience? To discover that he liked spending time on a farm more than he'd ever thought possible? That there was life beyond fighting for his country?

A shiver tripped down Max's spine. He wasn't the type to shiver or believe in fate or portents or anything else. But just thinking that thought, that Dad wanted him to discover a life beyond the Navy and the Special Ops world he lived in, affected him somewhere deep inside. Because until now, he hadn't considered that Dad thought anything about what he did beyond being proud of him for it.

If Dad was meddling in some way... Well, Max would make up his own mind about what was good for him. Max determined his future, not his father—and not from beyond the grave.

"Thanks, Aunt Claire. Give my love to Laurel and Hannah," he added. He hadn't talked to his cousins in forever, but he thought of them fondly.

"I will, honey. And you tell Mary Lou I still remember her derby pie with great fondness the next time you see her.

Have her make you a Kentucky hot brown sometime, if you haven't already."

He didn't even know what that was. He'd probably seen it on the menu but hadn't read the description. "Not yet, but I will."

"All right. Bye, sweetie."

He walked out of the bedroom and into the living room. The ceilings were tall and the furniture was old, but there were built-ins and a fireplace. He could see the room stripped of furnishings and repainted, could see the new life it could have. Cozy nights by the fireplace with Ellie...

Max shivered again as he headed out of the room and went to stand outside on the front porch. It was wide and long and could hold outdoor furniture for sitting and sipping drinks.

Jesus, what the hell? Max got out his keys and stood there, flipping them around his fingers until he heard the door open.

"Sorry," Ellie said as she locked up. "Lacey called and I had to take it."

His protective instincts went into overdrive. "Everything okay? Brice didn't harass her, did he?"

"Oh no, she's fine. But I wanted to make sure, so I had to answer."

"Understood."

Ellie smiled, and his world tipped on its axis. *No, this is* not *happening. You like her, and that's all.*

"You still taking me to Malone's?"

"If that's where you want to go."

"Then let's get moving. I'm starved!"

The nervousness Ellie had felt around Max earlier in the barn had disappeared when he'd emerged from the shower clad in a towel and taken her in his arms. All through the time they'd spent exploring each other, making each other crazy, and then losing themselves in the sweetness of release, she hadn't felt an ounce of nerves.

But ever since she'd walked out on the porch and found him waiting for her, she was back into jumpy territory. They'd taken his truck, and she'd pointed out farms along the way. She got a kick out of his reaction to the Castle Post Hotel on the way to Lexington. Most people had a hard time believing there was a medieval castle on a hill in Kentucky, but there it was, complete with stone walls and towers and a central "keep" that housed the hotel.

They continued on their way, past the airport and Keeneland, and sat down in Malone's a good twenty minutes later. Malone's was popular and crowded, but they got a booth at the back and Ellie ordered her steak along with the bottomless Lexingtonian salad and the mac and cheese. Max ordered a steak too. He seemed a little reserved, and that only made her more nervous. He hadn't been reserved when he'd had his mouth and hands all over her earlier.

Finally, when they'd been served their salads and bread and the conversation was sputtering along, she decided she'd had enough. Her nerves were stretched thin anyway, so she went for broke. "What's the matter, Max?"

Because she didn't like being on edge, and she wasn't going to let him do that to her.

He frowned as he looked up from his salad. "What makes you think something's wrong?"

She spread her hands, palms up. "You aren't exactly chatty tonight."

"I'm never chatty."

"Fine. You aren't chatty. But you do hold up your end of the conversation. You aren't doing that."

He toyed with his knife. "I'm sorry. My aunt called before we left. I've been thinking about some things she said."

That gave her pause. "I hope nothing's wrong at home."

"No, everything's fine. She didn't know your mother had died, by the way. She sends her condolences."

Ellie's throat was tight. "Thank you."

He put down his fork and knife. "I don't know why my dad left me your farm, Ellie. I think—on some level I think he was trying to direct my choices in life. But he can't do that. He can't change who I am or what's important to me by giving me something I know nothing about."

Ellie tried to smile. "You know more now than you did a week ago."

"I do… but it's not me, Ellie. Horses, the farm, living a quiet life in Kentucky—it's not me. It's not who I am or what I do."

There was a knot in her belly. "No one said it had to be, did they? You're here, trying to convince me to sell and learning how we operate while you do that."

"I'm not going to ask you to sell. Not anymore."

He'd said earlier that he wasn't going to take the farm from her, and while it had made her heart leap, she'd also been worried about him and what he wanted. Because if he didn't have the money from the farm, he would have to put

off his dream—which meant he'd go back to doing dangerous things. Or more dangerous things than what he wanted to
do with his own business. She had to assume that was less
risky than what he did now, which was certainly a powerful
motivation to make that change.

"I'll get the money, Max. Champ will win at Louisville
and I'll get an offer. And even if he doesn't win, I'll get an
offer because everyone is going to know how very good he
could be with the right trainer once they see him. Everything
will work out, and we'll both get what we want. You can stay
here until then if you like. No pressure."

But her belly churned and her skin prickled with heat.
Not the heat of arousal or need, but worry. She worried about
Champ performing well next week because that could set the
tone for the season, and she worried about Max, about what
he was going to do. And she didn't want him to go. There it
was—she didn't want him to leave when she was just now
getting to know him. She liked having him around—liked the
way he looked at her, the way he touched her, the way she
felt when he was buried inside her. It was different with him.
She felt things she'd never felt before, and maybe that was
her inexperience and the fact she'd never encountered a man
like him—a man who was so sexy and in charge, who knew
what he wanted and took it, who inspired confidence in his
ability to get things done just by the tone of his voice and the
way he attacked a problem.

"I know," he said. "And thanks. But Ellie, don't sell
yourself short, okay? Lacey and Miguel say that horse is one
of the best they've ever seen. He didn't get that way by himself."

Their steaks arrived then, and she couldn't say anything until the waiter walked away. "No, he didn't, but someone with more experience could take him further."

"How does a horse trainer get more experience, Ellie?"

He'd arched an eyebrow and was looking at her with a challenging expression. Now that was more like the Max she expected. The Max she'd lived with for the past several days.

"It takes time. You get there by training and showing and working hard—and having a good mentor."

"Your mother was your mentor, am I right?"

"She was."

"And was she good?"

Pride swelled Ellie's chest. "One of the best. She trained four world's champions—though we never had a world's *grand* champion."

"Then you be the one to get that brass ring," he said. "Don't give up until you get it."

"It takes years," she said.

"You got anything else to do?"

She couldn't help but grin. "No."

"Exactly."

Impulsively, she reached across the table and grabbed his hand. He didn't pull away. "Come to the show next weekend and watch Champ work. It's his first show, and I could use the moral support."

She saw the hesitation flash through his eyes, as if he was considering not being in Kentucky at all. As if he was planning to take that job in the desert and leave anyway. But then he squeezed her hand and nodded. "I'll be there."

Relief washed through her then, so strong she felt weak with it. She picked up her fork and kept eating. She had no idea what was going on here, not really, but whatever it was, it twisted up her insides and made her jumpy as a cat. She liked this man far too much for comfort—but she didn't think he felt the same.

She didn't blame him. He hadn't twisted her arm or anything. He'd warned her, in fact. Told her he had nothing to offer her, but she'd barreled forward anyway, refusing to walk away when he told her she should.

And now they were lovers. Every day that passed, she felt drawn deeper into the mire of her emotions. Since the night he'd sat with her in the barn, if she was honest with herself, that's when she'd started to feel more than she should. It was too late to change it. All she could do was ride it out until the end.

And pray her heart survived.

CHAPTER SEVENTEEN

Max couldn't sleep. He sat on the porch for the second time tonight. Earlier, he and Ellie had come home from Lexington and sat out here. She had a glass of wine, he had a beer. They talked. Nothing so deep as what they'd talked about earlier. Nothing about his dad or her mom or the future of the farm. It was mostly stories about growing up—her with horses, him as the son of a successful tycoon. To say they'd led disparate lives was an understatement.

And yet they were connected, not only by the fact his father had left him this farm but by the relationship between their mothers. His mother had loved this place, he had no doubt. He didn't have to hear it from anyone's lips to know it. The picture of her on a horse with Pam at her side was enough evidence. The smiles, the sheer happiness on their faces, the look of utter contentment.

He saw that look on Ellie's face when she was with her horses. She loved those beasts, and it kind of surprised him to realize his mother had too. But she'd given it up. For love, for kids, for whatever reason. Some people walked away from horses and never went back. But many did. Ellie had told him about her newest student, Terri. A woman who'd ridden twenty years ago but then marriage and family got in the way.

The kids were in high school now, and Terri missed riding. So she'd returned to it and she was even talking about buying her own horse. Ellie hoped she would. She had a good seat, Ellie said. Whatever that meant.

They'd ended up in bed, of course. He'd taken her to his room, made love to her on the air mattress with the smell of fresh paint hanging in the air in spite of the fact he'd opened the windows. She'd marveled at the windows, and he'd promised to get the rest of them open. Old houses and windows that were painted shut. It was practically a requirement.

And then she'd fallen asleep in his arms, curled around him, and he'd lain there awake, feeling both content and restless at the same time. He hadn't meant to take her to bed again. He'd told himself after the conversation with Aunt Claire that he needed to back off and figure out what he had to do next.

He enjoyed Ellie, there was no doubt. But it wasn't fair to her to let this keep going if there was no future in it. And there wasn't, because that wasn't him. Wasn't his life.

Yet every time he thought that, he got a pinch in his chest, as if someone were stabbing him with a very sharp, very thin knife. He liked her too much. And part of him liked this life, which was so uncomplicated compared to what he usually did.

Like now, sitting in the dark on this porch. It was comforting. He had time to think. Not the kind of thinking he did on watch when lives were on the line, but thinking about anything and everything.

Thinking about the best place to put a master bath addition. Thinking about refinished floors and freshly painted walls, about wood restored and wiring redone.

Jesus, what the hell was wrong with him?

He stood and started down the steps, needing to walk in the cool grass and clear his mind. He headed for the barn, because that was the most logical place to go. It wasn't quiet out here, far from it. There were crickets and frogs and the sound of horses softly moving in the grass from time to time.

He heard the sound of an engine in the distance, but that wasn't entirely unusual. The road was a few hundred feet away, and traffic sometimes passed this late at night. He kept going, kept thinking. He was halfway to the barn when a shot cracked in the relative stillness. He froze, his blood running cold. It wasn't deer season. Another farmer could be shooting at coyotes perhaps. But then horses' hooves pounded in the night, and he knew that no one was shooting at coyotes. There was neighing and frightened snorting, and another shot sounded.

A high-pitched whinny sounded then, and Max broke into a run. He didn't have a weapon, but he didn't necessarily need one. Most people would go the other way, but he ran toward the sound of the shots, leaping over the fence and into the pasture. They were coming from the other side of the field, and he ran hard toward the last location, keeping as low as he could while also staying away from the horses, which seemed to be a target for whomever was shooting.

It could be kids. Teenagers did stupid things sometimes. Or it could be worse. A horse snorted and neighed, and Max feared the worst. But he had to catch the culprit. That was his one thought. Catch the asshole and take him down hard.

A vehicle engine revved and then roared into the night. Max kept running as taillights appeared when the driver tapped the brakes. Then the headlights flashed on and the vehicle accelerated down a path that ran along the pasture before disappearing into the woods.

Whoever it was would get away, there was no doubt about that, but Max kept running anyway. And then there was the sound of squealing brakes and a crash as the vehicle plowed into something. Max redoubled his efforts and kept running.

A truck had crashed into a fence just a few yards ahead as the driver misjudged the turn and skidded headlong into the barrier. The engine whined as the driver tried to back up and get free. Max threw himself at the driver's side door, wrenching it open. A male voice yelled obscenities at him and a handgun swung into view. Max didn't hesitate as he swiftly disarmed the man and then dragged him from the truck by the throat and slammed him into the ground.

The driver hit with a thud but tried to get up again. Max dropped him with a blow and he was still, his hands rising to shield his face as if he expected another blow.

"What the hell?"

It was Ellie's voice. Max turned to see her approaching with a shotgun in her hands and a wild-eyed look on her face. She must have woken when the shots sounded. She came closer and then she shined a flashlight on the man lying in the grass. He blinked and groaned and Max wanted to kick him again just on principle.

"Brice Parker. You *asshole*," Ellie hissed. "If you hurt any of my horses, I'm going to fucking shoot you myself."

Max reached down and lifted Brice by his throat. He

made choking noises as his legs kicked helplessly.

"I warned you, didn't I?" Max growled. "I told you what I'd do if you came near Ellie or Lacey ever again."

Brice sniveled like the pussy he was. "Let me go. I didn't do anything wrong. Please."

"Shut up, asshole. Ellie, call the police before I kill this motherfucker for breathing."

Ellie took out her cell phone and made the call. Max shoved Brice against the side of the truck and then reached inside and pulled out a box of 22-caliber rifle shells. A peek in the back of the truck would no doubt reveal the rifle. "What the hell were you hunting, asshole?"

Brice spit in the grass. The truck's engine idled, and Hank Williams spilled from the radio. "Nothing. It's a free country."

"Not when you hunt Ellie's horses, it's not."

Ellie finished the call. Her face was white in the light filtering down from the trees. The moon was coming up and illuminating the landscape, and Max's heart hurt for her. If one of those horses was hurt, she'd be devastated. Considering the sounds he'd heard earlier, he suspected one was. The fact he heard nothing now worried him. Had one of her horses died?

"Did you hit any of my horses?" she growled as she walked over to them.

"I didn't shoot any horses," Brice said.

"You had better damned well hope not," Ellie snarled at him.

"Go," Max told her. "Check the pasture."

"As soon as the police arrive."

"Ellie," Max said. "It's okay. I can handle it."

She seemed to hesitate. And then she thrust her shotgun at him. "Take this."

He didn't need it, but he took it anyway. Probably for the best, because if she found any of her horses dead in that pasture, she was coming back to kill this man.

Max thought he might just help her, if so.

Ellie's gut twisted as she ran the flashlight over her horses. Lily had been hit. Blood dripped from a hole in her hindquarters while she shivered. The baby was fine, but he stayed close to his momma. Ellie soothed the mare with soft words as she walked up slowly. She got ahold of the halter and led the horse toward the barn. The baby followed while the other horses snorted and pranced a short distance away.

Ellie dialed the emergency vet while she walked, her fingers shaking hard. He answered on the second ring and she told him what happened. She heard sirens in the distance as the police made their way to the farm. She thought of Max holding Brice at gunpoint and knew there was no way the asshole was getting away with this.

Small comfort at the moment, but at least it was something. When the vet arrived, the police were everywhere. He tended to Lily while Ellie stayed close by. A cop came to talk to her while she held the mare.

"She'll be fine," the vet said when he finished. He left instructions and medicine, and Miguel showed up to watch over everything while Ellie went down to the police station with Max. He'd walked up in the blue glare of the lights, his face an angry mask, and her heart had skipped with gratitude. And maybe something more, though she was too tired to know what that was. They'd ridden in silence to the station, and then they'd been separated, presumably to give their version of events in their statements. By the time they were ready to leave, it was after six a.m.

"I'm sorry, Ellie," Max said as he drove her back to the farm.

"It's not your fault. You caught him. I don't even want to think of the danger you put yourself in to do it either."

"I know what I'm doing. It was fine. But I'm sorry he did such a terrible thing and hurt one of the horses." His voice was low and filled with anger, and she reached out to squeeze his arm.

"Thank you. Lily will be okay—and her baby is unharmed. If he'd just waited until the moon was up... Well, I shudder to think of it. Even though it was only a .22, he could have killed her if he'd taken good aim and hit her in the right spot. Or he could have killed the baby." She sounded perfectly calm, but inside she was screaming.

"He's an idiot," Max growled. "He wanted to hurt you, but he didn't plan it well."

"Thank God."

"Agreed."

She could tell that Brice's attack on the animals had hit a nerve with Max. It had hit a nerve with her too, of course, but she was surprised at how angry Max was. Considering the kinds of things he must have seen as a SEAL and as a contract soldier—or whatever it was he did—she had to think that a redneck trying to shoot horses was pretty low on the scale of violence and misery he was accustomed to.

"I watched him," he said. "I followed him and watched —and I didn't see this coming."

She gaped at him. He'd followed Brice? "I don't understand. When?"

He threw her a glance. "After Lacey filed the restraining order. I watched him to see if he'd go near her. I didn't trust that he wouldn't, and I didn't want to leave her unprotected."

Understanding dawned. Those nights after Lacey had gone home when she'd wondered where Max was. She'd thought he was avoiding her, but he'd been protecting Lacey. Her heart swelled with so many feelings that she couldn't quite deal with them all. Not yet.

"You kept Lacey safe."

"But I didn't keep you safe."

"I'm fine, Max. My horses are fine—mostly fine. The vet says Lily will recover quickly. The bullet wound isn't life threatening. Am I pissed beyond belief that it happened? Hell yes I am. But not at you. How could you know he'd come after me?"

"I should have known. When he didn't go near Lacey, when he avoided calling or following her—I should have realized he'd shifted his target. A man like that is too used to getting what he wants to ever let go of an insult so easily. I insulted him, and Lacey complicated matters with the restraining order. That left you. He wouldn't come after you, but he knew he could hurt you if he harmed your horses."

Ellie shuddered. "It could have been worse. He could have set the barn on fire."

"Too risky. He wanted the distance and anonymity a drive-by shooting would provide."

"Thankfully, it didn't work out, and everyone in town

will know what he did by tonight."

"Yep."

They turned into the farm then and eased down the drive. Soon she'd have to go help Miguel and prepare for the day. Even though she was exhausted, she had to work or lose revenue. And with a show coming next week, she needed every extra dollar she could get. As it was, she was going have to sell a kidney to finance this show season.

Or maybe a horse.

"I'm so grateful you were here, Max. I don't know what I'd have done without you. What Lacey would have done. You're—" She choked because she didn't know quite what to say. *Amazing? Incredible? The most wonderful man I've ever met?*

Somehow, she didn't think those were the appropriate things to say just now. She was tired and emotionally wrung out and she was second-guessing everything. He looked over at her, and she knew she had to say something.

"You're a good friend," she said, her heart hammering. She wanted to slap her hands over her face and hide. Gah, how lame was that? Friend? He was so much more.

He smiled at her and she felt like maybe—just maybe—that had been an okay thing to say. "Thanks."

They pulled up to the barn, and he put the truck into park. When he turned to her, his eyebrows were drawn low and he looked very serious. So serious that her heart skipped a beat.

"I won't leave you shorthanded, Ellie—but I think it's probably time I think about getting back to what I'm good at and leave you to do what you're good at. I've learned all I need to know about the farm."

She wanted to grab him and refuse to let him go. "If that's what you feel is best."

Because what else was she supposed to say? Please, please, please don't go? Please stay here and don't leave me, not yet? But she wouldn't say any of those things.

His nod was curt. "I think it might be. Brice Parker isn't going to be a threat ever again—not after the damage this is going to do to his business—and my skills are needed elsewhere."

She knew he was right, but disappointment still seized her. He wanted to leave. After everything. She'd thought—

Well, it didn't matter what she'd thought. He'd told her not to expect anything, hadn't he? He wasn't any different than Dave. Or her father. Men who hung around while it was convenient for them but then left when they were done. Dave had walked out, leaving her to pick up the pieces and move on. She'd done so during one of the toughest times in her life. Doing so now, compared to then, was going to be a piece of proverbial cake.

Ellie swung the door open and stepped out. Max just stared at her. She pasted on her best smile. "I hate to see you go, but if you must, then you must. Just let me know where to send the payments, okay? I've been sending them to your father's lawyer, same as always, but if you want them somewhere else, I can do that."

His frown was hard. "That's fine."

"Okay. Well, I have work to do now. Will you be leaving today?" She was on autopilot. It was the only explanation for how she could stand there and hold such a civil conversation when her heart was breaking inside. She didn't know why it hurt so much, but oh my heaven, it most certainly did.

"Not today, no. I have to make some arrangements first."

"If those arrangements are for me, don't bother. I'm fine. Miguel and Lacey are here, same as always. I've appreciated the help, but I can't afford to pay anyone else anyway, so it doesn't matter."

His gaze was impenetrable. Unreadable. "Are you saying you want me to go as soon as possible?"

"You've decided you're going, so go. Don't hang around and make me care even more than I already do. I've had enough disappointments in my life. I don't need another one."

She slammed the door and hurried into the barn before he could reply, her eyes blurring with tears. She was so angry, damn him. How dare he come here and make her care about him, then decide he'd had enough and it was time to go? He'd come to take her farm away, but even if he wasn't doing that anymore, she didn't feel like she'd won a damn thing.

She felt hollow and empty, like a used-up husk. This moment was supposed to be a triumph—he wasn't forcing her to sell, and though he hadn't said it, she was positive he wouldn't sell it out from under her when September came. But all she could feel was a crushing sense of loneliness. And as if she'd just lost everything that mattered.

Max called Ian Black and informed him he'd be in country in two days. Then he called and arranged for the dumpster to be picked up. He spent the next few hours unsticking as many windows as he could because he'd told Ellie he would.

He ignored the pervasive ache in his chest that got worse as the day went on. He couldn't stop thinking of Ellie's face this morning when he'd dropped her at the barn. She'd looked tired and lonely and... disappointed. Yeah, that was the word. She looked as if he'd disappointed her, and that bothered him on a deeper level than he'd expected.

When lunch came, she drove off with Lacey. Max watched Lacey's Honda roll down the drive, leaving a trail of dust in her wake. Then he went back to what he was doing, which was shoving his clothes into the duffel so he could get in the truck and drive away.

A distant part of his brain couldn't quite believe he was doing this. It kept asking him how he'd gotten into this mess and how he'd managed to maneuver himself into such a position that he had to go. Not only go, but go *today*.

Goddammit, he didn't know. One minute, he'd been enjoying Ellie and the temporary life he was leading here on the farm, and the next, he was questioning everything. Why had Dad left him Applegate Farm? Was Colin Brannigan trying to manipulate his sons from beyond the grave?

Luke, Gabe, Hunter, and Knox were all either married or getting married, and that was not a state of affairs to which Max aspired. He liked Ellie, but dammit, if he stayed here and kept sharing her bed... Well, she'd expect something more eventually, no matter that he'd told her he had nothing to give, and that was not fair to her. She was a good woman, and she didn't need his brand of insanity in her life. She'd been through too much already.

They were too different. She knew what her life was

supposed to be, where she wanted to be, and what she was doing. Applegate Farm was her life. His life was mud and blood and conflict. Even if he opened his protection firm, he'd still be traveling to hot spots and putting himself in danger on a regular basis.

That distant part of him asked why he couldn't open a personal-security firm here in Kentucky. While he'd been here, he'd learned a lot about the area. Lexington was filled with wealthy people who came to buy horses or who lived here and raised racehorses. He'd been told that when the sales happened at Keeneland or the Breeders' Cup was going on, the number of private jets sitting at the airport rivaled the traffic at Atlanta's Hartsfield-Jackson International Airport on any given day. Many of them were foreign too.

And all those people needed some sort of personal-security arrangements. They probably brought security with them—but if they could hire someone in the local area, someone with a firm that had an excellent reputation and the highest recommendations?

Max shook his head. Personal security for billionaires at the races wasn't his deal. His skills were more lethal than that, more specialized. He'd miss the excitement of the life he'd built during and after the Navy. He was a former SEAL, not a bodyguard. And yeah, there was a difference even with the high-end protection firm he visualized. He and his people weren't going to be bodyguards in the conventional sense.

But what's wrong with that? What's wrong with a quieter existence? What's wrong with life beyond Special Ops?

Max stiffened as that thought crossed his mind. It's what Dad wanted for him, not what he wanted. And he wasn't going to do what Dad wanted just because Dad wanted to manipulate him into it. If his father had been concerned about what Max chose to do with his life, maybe he should have been around more when Max and his brothers were kids.

He shouldered the duffel and took one last look around. Then he went outside and threw his bag in the truck. Miguel's truck was at the barn. Max hesitated for a moment, then went down to say good-bye. He found Miguel bringing in a load of shavings for a freshly mucked stall, and his guilty conscience pricked him. Hard.

Miguel didn't turn off the tractor, but he did throttle it down to idle speed. His expression wasn't friendly like it usually was. Still, he stuck his hand out and shook Max's when Max offered.

"It was nice to meet you, Max."

"You too, Miguel. Thanks for all the help."

"Yes." Miguel started to drive away, then lowered the throttle back to idle. "I think you are different. I meet you and I think, this man, he the one to help Ellie. But now you go, and I think how can I be so wrong."

Max put his hands in his jeans pockets. "I'm going to help her, Miguel. But I don't have to stay to do it. I have my own life— And, well, it's best I go."

"She upset. I can see it."

"Brice Parker shot one of her horses. Of course she's upset."

"It's more than Brice. It's you. She like you. I thought you like her."

Max's chest ached. "I do like her. But I can't stay. We're too different, and I'll only screw things up if I stay. She needs to concentrate on Champ and the farm. And she deserves a guy who likes all the same things she does."

Miguel snorted. "My wife likes knitting. I know nothing of this. I don't care to know anything. We seem fine in spite of my inability to love yarn."

"You're a good guy, Miguel. I won't forget you."

Miguel's expression fell. "Fine. You go. Maybe you change your mind when you see how much you miss us here."

Max grinned. "Maybe I will."

He went and got in the truck, letting his gaze slide over the fields and fences one last time. The horses were grazing, the sunlight streaming down on glossy coats, and babies romped in the grass. Thank God Brice Parker wasn't a great shot. He wouldn't try again, that's for sure. His ass was about to be embroiled in litigation for the foreseeable future. Still, Max would put in a call, make sure that Brice knew the consequences of ever attempting to harm Ellie or anyone, person or animal, that she loved ever again.

Max knew some bad motherfuckers. He had no problem calling in a favor or two if it protected Ellie.

Max thought of James's advice to put the farm on the market regardless of what Ellie thought. Of course there'd been no way he would have ever done that.

But there was something else he could do. He couldn't stay here with Ellie, couldn't be what she needed in the long term—but he could do something even better. Something that would ensure her happiness forever.

CHAPTER EIGHTEEN

Ellie answered her phone when she saw it was Janet calling. She was giving a lesson, but the kid was still saddling the horse, and she had a few moments before she had to instruct. She'd been keeping busy since Max left, but she knew every single moment that had passed between then and now no matter how hard she tried not to think about it. He'd been gone for a week, and she'd heard nothing from him. Not that she'd expected to.

Still, it didn't stop her from snatching up her phone the second it buzzed or dinged, hoping it was him.

Disappointment gnawed at her. "Hi, Janet. What's up?"

"Ellie—I need you to come into the office today. Can you do that?"

Ellie frowned. "I can—but not for another couple of hours. Why?"

"It's better if we talk in person."

"Does this have anything to do with Brice?" Because, God help her, if he ever showed his ass anywhere near her farm again, she was unloading both barrels on him. He was out on bail, but things were not looking so good for him according to Janet. Unless something had changed, which made Ellie's insides clench tight.

"No, it's not Brice. He's still in a heap of trouble and keeping himself squeaky clean while his lawyer tries to cop a plea deal with the DA's office. He will definitely not bother you ever again, especially once he writes a check for damages."

"You mean for Lily's pain and suffering." Janet had suggested she sue Brice in the first place. She was grateful for it, and she meant to carry on with the suit, if for no other reason than to make sure Brice never messed with her or her loved ones ever again.

"I know, honey. The law looks at it like damages to property though."

Ellie sighed. "Can you give me a hint?"

"Bring your checkbook."

With that cryptic phrase, they ended the call and Ellie gave a lesson. Then she did a few things around the barn before climbing into her truck and driving the short distance into town. Janet was waiting and stood excitedly when her secretary showed Ellie in.

Ellie couldn't imagine what was going on as she went over and sat down in front of Janet. Janet took her seat again, opened a folder, and turned it toward Ellie.

Ellie looked at the contract sitting there and frowned. "What is this?"

"It's a contract to sell Applegate Farm. To *you*, Ellie. The Brannigan lawyers sent it over this morning."

Ellie's breath stopped in her throat. She flipped the pages of the contract to the very end. There was a place for her signature. Max's signature hadn't been filled in yet.

"How much?" She had to force the words out. Her temples throbbed and her heart raced.

Janet's smile was positively gleeful. "One dollar."

Ellie reared back in her chair as her stomach dropped and her heart soared at the same time. "Did you say... one *dollar?*"

Janet nodded. "That's what I said. Max Brannigan wants to sell Applegate Farm to you for a dollar. All you have to do is write a check and sign the paperwork. He'll cosign, the deed will be recorded, and you own your farm again, Ellie."

If she were a weaker person, she'd be sobbing right now. As it was, she barely prevented it from happening. Her throat hurt and her eyes stung. *Max, what have you done?*

"You won't have to sell Champ if you don't want to. You won't have to do anything but build Applegate Farm into the powerhouse it used to be. Ellie, this is *good* news."

"I know it is." She felt like she was talking around razor blades in her throat.

"Then why do you look like he sold the farm to someone else? Ellie, this is your dream come true! It's better than your dream."

Possibilities whirled in her head. Applegate Farm, free and clear. Champ wouldn't need to be sold. He'd stay hers to show and breed. More clients, more horses, more help. A vibrant and self-sustaining working farm. Because they could get there, she knew they could. No, this wasn't a magic pill—but it was the beginning of everything.

It was also the end of Max's dream, at least for the next five years. How could he do it? *Why* did he do it?

Ellie sat there, staring at the contract and asking herself a million questions. More than anything, she wanted to know why. She missed him so much that it hurt, but she was working on getting over that.

And then he went and did this, and her heart cracked wide open again. She loved who he was as a person even while she didn't understand him. She pressed a hand to her mouth as she took that thought a step further.

She loved *him*. She loved Max Brannigan. Somehow, some way, he'd gotten under her skin and she'd fallen for him. She hadn't meant to, but she had. It was too late to change it.

But she could change this. She could refuse to accept his gift, because if she took it, if she accepted her dream at the expense of his... Well, what did that say about *her?* About what kind of person *she* was?

She pushed the contract back and stood. "I'm not signing that, Janet."

Her friend looked stunned. "What do you mean, you aren't signing it? It's everything you wanted, Ellie!"

She drew herself up, shaking from head to toe, her heart throbbing with love and misery all at once. "No, it's really not. Tell them no deal. I'll keep paying the way I always have."

Janet was on her feet as Ellie turned to the door. "If you don't take this deal—Ellie, he can sell the farm in September and you'll have nothing."

Ellie put her hand on the door knob. "I know he can. But he won't."

She left Janet staring at her like she was crazy and went outside to climb into her truck. She had a show to get ready for and no time to worry about the *what-ifs*.

Max was pissed. He'd been in Acamar for four days, and now he was on the way out again.

A week ago he'd driven back to DC, boarded the plane for Acamar, and then spent the next fifteen hours or so brooding about life. He'd sat on the plane missing Ellie and the horses—missing horses?—for hours. He'd thought of everything they'd said and done together, and then he'd thought of everything they'd said to each other that final time. She'd had those two splotches of color in her cheeks as she'd told him he needed to go if he was going, and he'd stubbornly done just that.

Before he'd gone, however, he'd made the decision to return the farm to her. The contract his father had left stipulated that the price at which he sold it to her, if he sold it to her, was up to him. So he sold it for a dollar. Trent Harper, his dad's attorney, had nearly gone apeshit. Max hated to think what James would have said, so he didn't call his eldest brother at all.

In fact, he'd called no one other than Trent when he'd decided to do it. It was between him and Ellie. He didn't want her to worry anymore, and he didn't want her to have to sell Champ to the highest bidder. He'd seen how much she loved her horses. If he hadn't known it before, the way she'd gone all momma bear over Lily would have told him that.

She cared about their welfare, and if she were forced to hand Champ over to the highest bidder to keep her farm going... Well, who knows what kind of a person he could end up with?

Yeah, you'd think someone who paid a lot of money for a horse would take care of it—but would he be loved and pampered the way he was at Applegate Farm? Those were the kinds of things Ellie would worry about, no doubt.

So Max had gotten to Acamar and gone to work. He knew it would take time for the contract to be drawn up, but he'd had no doubt she'd sign it. He'd been embedded with a unit deep in the desert when he'd gotten a call from Ian Black. He had a special cell phone for the mission, not his personal one, so Ian was the only one who could call.

"Your attorney keeps calling me and won't let up. He says, and I quote, 'She didn't take the deal. Please advise.'"

Max had spent about six hours telling himself it didn't matter before he called Ian back and said he had to get back to the States. There'd been little action in Acamar, and they were basically sitting around with their thumbs up their asses anyway. The action they'd expected hadn't happened. Not that it wouldn't, but so far it was a lot of sitting and waiting. And thinking, because Max couldn't stop thinking if he wasn't immediately fighting for his life or rescuing hostages.

"I suspected that. You didn't seem to have your heart in it this time anyway."

"What's that supposed to mean?"

"It means that I know when an operator is in it for the love of what he's doing, or for the adrenaline rush, or even just the money. And I know when he's not. Whatever your reasons before, they aren't there right now."

210

No, they weren't. He didn't know what the hell was happening to him, but right now all he could think about was Ellie and why she didn't take his gift to her. What the fuck was she thinking?

So he got on a plane and rewound the trip. Sixteen hours back to DC, a quick overnight in his tiny apartment that didn't feel like anything but a place to store some stuff, and then on the road to Kentucky. When he turned into the drive at the farm, his gut was churning. But as he drove up to the house, he realized her truck and trailer weren't there.

Miguel was at the barn, however, and he stopped in his tracks as if he'd seen a ghost. Max ran a hand over his face, realizing he hadn't shaved in days. He hadn't had time.

"Where's Ellie?"

"She's at the show in Tennessee. Took a load over yesterday. She and Champ show tonight."

Son of a bitch.

"All right, guess I'm on my way to Tennessee then. You got a location?"

"Hang on." Miguel disappeared into the barn and then returned with a show flyer that had the date and time and location. There was a list of classes for each day and check marks beside the ones that presumably Ellie and her clients were riding in. "Show starts at six. Ellie's is the fifth class in. You might make it if you hurry."

Max started to shake Miguel's hand. Then he tugged the man forward and gave him a bro hug, slapping his back as he did so.

"Thanks, Miguel. I'm hurrying."

He climbed in the truck and Miguel called out. "You don't hurt Ellie again, you hear me? You don't want to know

211

what I will do to you. I no care if you are a big bad Navy SEAL. You have to sleep sometime."

Max laughed, feeling lighter than he had in days. "I hear you, brother."

He pointed the truck toward Tennessee and floored it.

Ellie was nervous. She was always nervous, even though she was supposed to know what she was doing. But she felt like her entire future rode on this moment. Like every dream she'd ever had would come down to six minutes in the ring. If Champ performed well, if he won, they were on the way to glory in Louisville.

And if he didn't, well, they still had work to do if they stood a chance of maximizing Champ's worth.

His coat was glossy beneath the lights. He was standing in his stall, munching hay, his saddle on and loosely girthed. She only had to bridle him and get on when it was time.

She'd already changed into her show clothes. All she had to do was put on the long coat, her derby, and tug on her gloves before mounting. She had to be careful not to get dirty, which was why she hadn't put them on yet. Plus it was hot.

Lacey was there to help, thank God. Lacey hadn't been sure if she could make this show, but then she'd shifted her client schedule and made it happen. She rode later tonight in the Country Pleasure class, so for now she could help Ellie. There were two other clients who'd come with them to the show, but neither of them rode tonight.

The voice over the loudspeaker announced which class was next and which was on deck. Ellie's stomach turned over as she realized her class would be on deck very soon.

"I'll bridle him." Lacey went into Champ's stall and took care of the bridle while Ellie put on the long, shiny navy coat and buttoned it before slipping on her hat and gloves. She took a look at herself in the mirror they'd set up in the tack room and sucked in a deep breath for courage.

When she walked out, Lacey had Champ in the aisle. He looked magnificent, but he also looked nervous. He was a young stallion, and there were mares here. He whinnied and Lacey shushed him.

Ellie dragged the mounting block over to his side and checked the girth. She tightened it another notch while Champ stood there like a good boy. When she stepped on the block, he danced sideways and tossed his head.

"He's excited," Lacey said.

"Easy boy," Ellie told him, moving the block again. This time she swung up with no problems, and Champ started to prance down the aisle. Lacey grabbed a towel and trotted alongside Ellie and Champ, wiping dust from Ellie's patent leather boots and doing a quick once-over of Champ's coat.

She handed up a whip and Ellie took it, gathering her reins a little more firmly and pushing Champ up and into the bridle. He was magnificent and excited, his nostrils blowing and ears swiveling, but he behaved once Ellie was on his back.

A few people stopped to look at them go by. This was a smaller show, but there were some big barns here. The kind of people who could buy Champ one day. She only hoped he made them take notice with his performance tonight. Ellie made it up to the practice arena, and Lacey unknotted Champ's tail where they'd tied it up to prevent it from getting dirty.

Ellie worked Champ at a trot to warm him up. After a few minutes, she set him up for a slow gait, that easy, smooth prequel to the fast rack. He performed it flawlessly, though he was a little strong tonight. She'd have to be careful in the arena or he could break over into a canter when he wasn't supposed to. And that could cost them the class if it happened.

She tried not to think about how important this was, but her nerves were certainly getting the best of her.

"Lacey!"

Lacey turned at the sound of the voice—and Ellie did too. Her heart skipped into overdrive, and she had to be careful not to jiggle the reins too much. Was that Max? Was it possible?

Lacey waved. "Max!"

Oh my God.

Max strode into the glow of the lights from the practice arena, and Ellie had to force herself to breathe. Lacey walked over to him and they hugged.

Was she dreaming? Hallucinating?

Then Lacey pointed at her, and Max climbed onto the lowest rung of the fence.

"You look beautiful, Ellie," he called out. "You and Champ both."

Champ danced, sensing her chaotic emotions. She directed him toward the fence. She had to keep him moving, but she had to see Max. His appearance shocked her. He was unshaven and looked like he'd been traveling for two days, but he looked so rugged and beautiful that she wanted to slip from Champ and throw her arms around him.

The announcer called for her class to get ready since the class currently in the arena was on the reverse. Champ was warm, but they probably needed another practice run around the warm-up area.

Still, she kept him moving toward Max.

"Why are you here?" she asked when she was close enough.

"I promised I'd be here, didn't I?"

"You did. But then you left."

"Yeah, well, I changed my mind."

She shook her head and rode Champ in a circle. "I can't talk right now. I have to get ready."

"I know," he said, smiling warmly. So warmly that her insides lit up, glowing just for him. "Knock 'em dead, Ellie. That's what you're here to do."

Champ was getting antsy, so she rode away from Max even while she didn't want to. She put him through his paces again, not too hard because she couldn't tire him out, and then she circled him at a walk. Max was gone when she looked, and disappointment sat like a stone in her belly. Lacey came over and handed up a bottle of water for a quick drink.

"He went inside to watch."

"Did you know he was coming?"

Lacey shook her head, her blond hair shining in the lights. "I had no idea—but it's great, isn't it? It must mean something if he came back."

"Maybe. Maybe not."

But she couldn't worry about it anymore because the announcer called her class.

"Showtime, buddy," she said to the horse rippling with energy beneath her. She cued him for a trot, and they sailed into the arena with all the future hopes and dreams of Applegate Farm riding on his hooves.

CHAPTER NINETEEN

M ax had never seen anything like what he saw in the arena that night. Ellie and Champ came trotting in like they were the best thing in the show—and they proved it too. There were eight horses in her class, and all of them were beautiful. But Champ was the prettiest one of all. And when they went into that rack thing they did?

Shit, there was nothing that could hold a candle to them. Champ flew faster than any of the others, his hooves striking the ground and flashing up high with every stride. He messed up at one point, but the judge wasn't looking. Another horse got too close and Champ swerved, breaking stride. Max didn't know much, but he knew it wasn't what they were supposed to be doing. But Ellie got him back quickly, and he kept flying around the arena to whoops, hollers, and yells of "Yeah, boy!"

When it was over and the horses were in the lineup, Max thought his heart was going to come out of his chest. He wanted Ellie to win. Wanted it so badly he could taste it—and when her number was called for first place, he was the first to yell for her.

Lacey went running into the ring with a towel. She wiped Champ off as someone pinned on a blue ribbon. They took a picture standing by the sign that named the show, and then there was a victory pass with the lights shining on the beautiful horse and the woman who looked so happy and confident sitting up there. People took notice of the pair—how could they not?

They passed out of the ring, and Max began the trek to the stables. Lacey had told him where they were, and he found them a few minutes later. Ellie was still in her gear, the long coat with the vest and tie, the derby hat, and shiny boots. She was peeling off her gloves and laughing at something Lacey said.

Max almost faltered at that point. He'd thought about Ellie a lot—on the way to Acamar, in Acamar, on the way back to DC, the long drive to Kentucky, and then the drive to Tennessee. And he knew something he hadn't known before.

She had his heart. Completely and utterly. He didn't know how it had happened, but it had. And it was too late to change it. He felt like an asshole for not realizing it sooner—and he was, for the first time in his adult life, afraid of something he couldn't control or tame.

He'd always thought love had ruined his father when his mother died. But that wasn't true. Love had saved him from who he was as a young man, transformed him into a good man with a wife and kids, and then left him sad and alone—but it hadn't ruined him. Hadn't abandoned him. It had shaped him and made him. Max knew in a way he never had before what his father was trying to do with this legacy.

He was trying to say, "I love you. I want you to find peace and happiness and figure out who you are. And only then will you be ready for a love of your own."

Jesus, that was sappy as shit—but it's what Max believed. Because there was no denying he was a changed man. No denying he'd do anything and everything to see this woman smile. He knew it in his bones.

She looked up then and saw him—and her smile faded. That gave him pause. But it didn't stop him from walking over to where she stood. She tilted her head back to gaze up at him questioningly. He wanted to touch her, but he refrained.

"You didn't buy the farm," he said.

"No, I didn't. Have you come to try to talk me into buying it? Or to tell me you plan to sell it anyway?"

He shook his head. Sell it? He was never selling it. "No. That offer is off the table."

She nodded. "All right. So what's the offer now?"

"That you let me give it to you for a wedding present."

She frowned, and then her lower lip trembled. "I... What? I'm not getting married."

"Not yet, no. But I hope you will. Someday. When you're ready."

She shook her head. "Max, you aren't making any sense."

Lacey gave an exaggerated sigh in the background. "El, you aren't *listening* to him. For heaven's sake, pay attention."

Max wanted to laugh. Lacey had his number. She'd had it for a while.

Ellie gazed up at him again. "Are you saying... Are you asking...?"

He couldn't help it. He tugged her into his arms, tilted her back, and kissed her. She melted in his embrace, her mouth softening beneath his, and he knew he was home.

"Yes," he said a short time later. "That's exactly what I'm asking."

"But I thought you didn't want this life. I thought we weren't what you needed."

"I'm an idiot, Ellie. I love you—and I missed the farm and these damned horses of yours. I missed Lacey and Miguel and the cats too. I missed Kentucky. I want to go home with you."

Her eyes were brimming with tears. "What about your dreams? That's why I couldn't buy the farm for a dollar, Max. You shouldn't have to wait five years to open your business."

"Dreams change. I want to renovate the house and help you turn Applegate Farm into the showplace you want it to be. And yeah, I'm going to start a business. But it'll be local, not global. I think there's plenty of business in Lexington to keep me busy for a while. Oh, and I want a dog too. Maybe a couple of them."

"Okay. I like dogs. And we'll sell Champ if it helps."

"We will not," he said. "Unless you want to for some reason, though I'd like to see you win that world's grand championship you were talking about someday. But no, I can start small with what I have. In a few years, it won't matter. I'm still a Brannigan, and I've still got a pretty big inheritance coming someday. You can show Champ to the pinnacle of success—and we'll build our own castle when I get money, if you want to."

She laughed. "I do not want a castle. There's only room for one of those in Versailles."

"Then there's only one thing left to say."

She smiled that soft, lovely smile of hers. "Yes, I'll marry you. I love you, Max Brannigan."

And that, he thought, was exactly how life was supposed to be. He would spend the rest of his life showing Ellie how he felt about her. And every day, when he walked through the bluegrass, he'd thank his dad for giving him a horse farm with fancy prancers instead of racehorses.

A place where he'd found himself when he didn't even know he was lost.

ACKNOWLEDGEMENTS AND NOTES

First, I have to thank the other authors in this project. Barbara Freethy, Ruth Cardello, Melody Anne, Christie Ridgway, Roxanne St. Claire, and JoAnn Ross were all so much fun to work with! When I had to decide what my hero was going to inherit as his bequest, it hit me pretty quickly that it was going to be a saddlebred farm. I couldn't think of anything more amusing than this big Special Ops guy inheriting fancy prancing horses.

I say that lovingly, by the way, because I own one of those fancy prancers. I grew up riding horses, mostly hunt seat and dressage, so when I accidently came back to horses as an adult after many years away, I did not expect to end up riding saddle seat at a saddlebred barn. Here's how it happened.

My mom, who has never been one to let the grass grow under her feet, decided she wanted to take up riding again. So she found a local barn where they just so happened to have saddlebreds and started going. She asked me for months to go meet everyone and see the horses (she had an ulterior motive, my husband says). Finally I cleared my schedule enough. I get out there and meet the trainer, who says to me, "What size boot do you wear?"

Once we got that out of the way, she found boots, a helmet, handed me a release form and said, "Now get on that horse." I did, and the rest is history. I've had a lot to learn about riding a saddlebred. A *lot*. I bought my horse, Reggie, after two months of going out there, and we haven't looked back.

Reggie's formal name is Roseridge's No Regrets. So, yes, Champ's name is inspired by Reggie. I couldn't quite call Champ Reggie in the story, because that seemed a little too overboard. Reggie is not a stallion, and though Reggie is five-gaited like Champ, he's not ever going to win a world's grand championship. I love him, but he isn't. ;)

Everything I know about saddlebreds I've learned in the past two years at B&W Stables. If I've gotten anything wrong in this book, it's not the fault of Joyce and Ken Webster or any of my wonderful barn family. I tried not to get it wrong, but for the sake of story and space, I've had to compress some things and leave out some details that horse people would probably love but others would not.

The horse names in this story are taken from horses in the barn. I even used a couple of them on the cats. I wish I could have included every horse at B&W, but I couldn't.

Thanks to Joyce and Ken, Liz and Webb, Regina and Joan, Colleen, Emily and Annette, Emily H., Sheila, Lindsey, Kelley, Joye, and my mom BJ for being the best barn family possible. Thanks to my husband Mike and my dad Mike for supporting us and going to horse shows with us even when they get bored and would rather be fishing.

As always, thanks to my team: Mike, Gretchen, Anne, Crystalle, Linda, Kelley, and Julie.

I hope you've enjoyed *Max*! If you want to learn more about saddlebreds, visit the American Saddlebred Horse Association at https://www.asha.net/.

ABOUT THE AUTHOR

Lynn Raye Harris is the *New York Times* and *USA Today* bestselling author of the HOSTILE OPERATIONS TEAM SERIES of military romances as well as 20 books for Harlequin Presents. A former finalist for the Romance Writers of America's Golden Heart Award and the National Readers Choice Award, Lynn lives in Alabama with her handsome former-military husband, two crazy cats, and one spoiled American Saddlebred horse. Lynn's books have been called "exceptional and emotional," "intense," and "sizzling." Lynn's books have sold over 3 million copies worldwide.

Connect with Lynn online:

Facebook: www.facebook.com/AuthorLynnRayeHarris
Twitter: https://twitter.com/LynnRayeHarris
Website: http://www.LynnRayeHarris.com
Email: lynn@lynnrayeharris.com

OTHER TITLES BY LYNN RAYE HARRIS

THE *HOSTILE OPERATIONS TEAM* SERIES

Prequel: Reckless Heat (Matt & Evie)

Book 1: Hot Pursuit (Matt & Evie)

Book 2: Hot Mess (Sam & Georgie)

Book 3: Hot Package (Billy & Olivia)

Book 4: Dangerously Hot (Kev & Lucky)

Book 5: Hot Shot (Jack & Gina)

Book 6: Hot Rebel (Nick & Victoria)

Book 7: Hot Ice (Garrett & Grace)

Book 8: Hot & Bothered (Ryan & Emily)

Book 9: Hot SEAL (Dane & Ivy)

Book 10: Hot Protector (Chase & Sophie)

57921261R00139

Made in the USA
Lexington, KY
28 November 2016